THE BROTHERS OF
BRIGADIER STATION

SARAH WILLIAMS

Serenade Publishing

Cover design: Lana Pecherczyk.

Pictures courtesy of iStock by Getty Images.

The Brothers of Brigadier Station / Sarah Williams. – 2nd ed. AUS English. KDP

ISBN 978-1-973111511

Serenade Publishing
www.serenadepublishing.com

❀ Created with Vellum

To Joshua
See, dreams do come true!

CHAPTER 1

*S*ettle down, boy." Meghan coaxed the huge German Shepherd, using all of her strength to keep the great beast on the cold, metal table.

"Almost done, just a little longer." Jennifer, the veterinarian, called from the end where the dog's great head lay as his owner watched.

Having your teeth checked at the dentist was never a pleasant experience, so Meghan couldn't blame the old dog for being agitated. She held chunks of its sweaty fur in her fists. It stank of dirt and urine. It had probably gotten anxious in the car ride and wet himself. Owners never told them that. It was common to find wet patches on the animals that visited Spotty Dogz Vet Surgery.

Still, in all her years working as a vet nurse, being wet on wasn't her worst experience. She was often a scratching post for vicious cats and had lost count of the numerous bites from a variety of rodents and birds.

Her pain threshold had increased dramatically since she had finished her training. There were other parts of the job that were far worse. Like caring for a cat who was in constant, agonizing pain or having an innocent young puppy die in her arms. Those experiences left a mark that couldn't be seen.

While healthy, domestic animals were cute and adorable, but it was the larger animals, especially horses, that Meghan wanted to work with.

"All done." Jennifer stepped back. The dog hurled itself out of Meghan's grasp and off the table. Claws scrapping on the metal surface.

Jennifer and the owner tackled the creature out of the room, leaving Meghan alone to clean the instruments and sterilize the table. After washing her hands, she visited her patients. A new litter of short haired, tabby kittens had been brought in after being found abandoned. Meghan had already checked the kittens for fleas and ticks when they had first arrived yesterday, now they were just waiting for microchipping and vaccinations. A brown and grey boy cried mournfully and Meghan couldn't help wishing she could adopt them all. She scooped up the tiny kitten and snuggled it against her chin. Its soft fur tickled her skin and its small heart thumped against her fingertips.

After a few minutes of loving, she placed the kitten back with his siblings, stroking all six in turn, saying a quiet goodbye and hoping they all found good homes before her next shift.

She sighed as she glanced at her watch, it was

almost the end of her shift. It had been a long day and she was looking forward to spending the night on the couch with her fiancé, Lachie. He had only arrived yesterday from his home in the outback and she had barely seen him yet.

Her phone buzzed in her back pocket. She pulled it out and answered when her best friend's name appeared.

"Hey, Jodie," a smile tugged at the corners of her mouth. Jodie could always make her feel better.

"Are you still at work?"

"Yeah. Almost over."

"I just wanted to wish you luck for tomorrow. What time are you leaving?"

"First thing. Lachie said it takes about seven hours plus breaks."

"Geez, what a long drive. Did you really have to fall for a guy who lives on a farm in the outback?"

Meghan laughed. "It's a cattle station, not a farm. It's been in the family for generations so he didn't get much of a choice where it was."

Jodie was quiet, but Meghan knew her friend well enough to know when she was rolling her eyes.

"Well, good luck meeting his family. Use these two weeks to make sure moving out there is what you really want."

"I will." Meghan's eyes prickled with threatening tears. "I'm going to miss you. We've been friends for what... twenty years? We've never been apart this long."

"It's going to be harder if you move out there permanently."

After the wedding, Meghan would call the station home. Leaving her best friend wouldn't be the only thing she would miss about Townsville. The beach, the food, the music. But the country promised excitement; a new start, a new identity, the family she longed for. She would become Mrs. Lachlan McGuire of Brigadier Station. She bit her lip, containing a grin. His country upbringing had been appealing right from the start. He was outgoing and confident. The fact that he was gorgeous helped too.

"Call me. I want updates. And photos. Find out about the other brothers. If either are single and hot, I want to know." Jodie was always keeping an eye out for her next boyfriend.

"I will. Love you."

"Love you too. Safe trip."

Meghan slipped her phone back in her trousers and glanced at her watch again. After her rounds, it would be time to say goodbye and her two-week holiday would start. She would finally meet Lachie's Mum and brother and see where he lived and had grown up. They would also be announcing their engagement.

At twenty-nine, Meghan Flanagan was about to have everything she had ever wanted. She was in love and moving to the country to start a new life. A better life. She had never been happier.

∾

The television was blaring when Meghan got home. The air smelled musty when she stepped into the kitchen. She placed the bags on the kitchen counter and opened a window, allowing a cool breeze to waft in. She peeked into her small living room. Lachlan McGuire was sprawled on the couch, beer in hand, watching the North Queensland Cowboys defend their title. He was relaxed and happy. She knew he liked spending time in her modest little house. Away from the station, he could ignore the paperwork and bills that were no doubt overloading his email account; he worked hard, so Meghan couldn't blame him wanting to take a break.

"What's the score?"

He looked up and grinned the grin that made her insides quiver. "Cowboys are up by twelve."

Cowboys games always reminded her of when she had met Lachie eight months earlier. Jodie had dragged her to a home game. By sheer good fortune, they had been seated next to each other. Lachie had quickly won her over with his good looks and charm. She had been surprised by the attention. Gorgeous guys didn't waste their time on plain girls like her. She wondered if he was being nice to her to get to Jodie. The tall, blonde beauty was often the centre of attention. But when the game was over, he asked for Meghan's number and within a week they were an item. Whenever she asked him why he had chosen her, he always replied: 'You're a girl I can take home to Mum.'

"Is that Thai food I smell?" He climbed off the couch and followed his nose to the kitchen.

"I got that Pad Thai you like." She watched as he opened containers appreciatively and started serving it up onto two plates.

Meghan moved into the sitting room, kicked off her shoes and curled up on the couch before turning the TV volume down with the remote.

"Did you do anything exciting today?" She called out as she waited for Lachie.

"Nah, just hung out here. Watched some TV." He carried the plates back to the living room to join her on the couch, balancing his plate on his knees.

"How was work?"

She shrugged. "I always liked my job, but now it's gotten so repetitive. I'm ready for a change."

"I reckon you'll love the country. Lots of wide open spaces and you're a country girl at heart." He winked at her before scooping a generous forkful of food into his mouth.

She had heard so much about their sprawling cattle property in the outback and his beloved mother.

"I'm nervous, I've never met a guy's Mum before."

"Mum's a treat. Don't be scared of her. Did you talk to Jodie today?"

"She called me at work and assured me it'll be okay."

"It will and this visit is only for a couple of weeks. After the wedding, we can still come visit once a year or so."

She looked into his blue eyes and smiled. Her future

was so full of hope and possibilities, it was exciting and a little frightening.

"I love you, Lachie. I can't wait to start our life together."

His lips brushed gently over hers causing warmth to pool in her belly.

She would meet his mother and brother tomorrow and she would finally see the property. Her future home.

Brigadier Station.

CHAPTER 2

*C*racked brown dirt stretched flat in every direction. The occasional ironbark tree provided the only shelter from the harsh elements of the North Queensland outback.

Although Meghan had never been this far from the coast before, she knew in her heart she would love the country and quickly adjust to living on the land. It had been a long drive from Townsville, passing through the small township of Charters Towers then the smaller, communities of Hughenden and Richmond. In these places, she had learnt of the abundant dinosaur fossils which were often found in the hard earth.

Now on the final stretch of dusty road between Julia Creek and Brigadier Station, she decided the stark, austere scenery was, surprisingly, quite beautiful.

"Don't worry," Lachie glanced at her as his ute rattled over a cattle-grid. "Brigadier isn't as bare as these stations. We've got plenty of shade and good bores.

"So, you're doing okay despite the drought?" Meghan had heard plenty of stories about how hard the outback graziers were doing it in this drought. Cattle were starving to death and many owners were killing their own stock rather than see their beasts suffer.

Lachie had grown up on the cattle station and had inherited it when his father died a few years ago. He had told her what to expect and she was more than up for the challenge.

"Well, we manage. It's not easy, though. Lots of hard work."

Meghan admired his profile. His trim and toned body were the result of that hard, physical work. The sleeves of his grey work shirt rolled up above his long, suntanned forearms. Meghan was shorter by a foot, but he towered over most people at his lofty six-foot-four height.

"What?" He caught her watching him. "You checking me out?"

She giggled flirtatiously. "So, what if I am?"

He wiggled his eyebrows at her. "I can always pull the ute over."

She crinkled her nose and gestured to the tools and machinery parts at her feet and between them.

"There's not enough room in here to move. Remember the last time we did it in here?"

His deep chuckle sent a shiver down her spine as it always did.

"Good point. But I do have my swag in the back." He gestured behind him to the tray, where her suitcase was tied down.

"That stinky old thing? I love you, but no thanks."

Winding the window down she let the warm air blow on her face, whipping her long hair about as they sped down the road. She gazed over the land, barren and deserted.

She hoped Lachie's family liked her. Especially his mum—a woman he admired and loved. Would she be hard and stern, like this land? Disappointed that her oldest son was with a city girl? Or would she be accepting and kind? Weren't country people supposed to be friendly?

"Don't be nervous."

She looked over and realised she had been gnawing on her bottom lip.

"That obvious?"

"There's no need. Mum will love you." He reached over and patted her knee briefly. "I'll tell her about the engagement at dinner. After she gets to know you a bit."

"I hope she approves." She rubbed her sweaty hands over her jeans. Lachie had proposed over pizza last weekend. It hadn't been a passionate gesture. He didn't even have a ring. But she had been delighted, throwing herself into his arms. That she might not be cut out for remote country life hadn't occurred to her. She loved the idea of wide-open space, animals, country quiet, and of course she loved Lachie.

They soon pulled into a gravelled driveway, marked only by a worn wooden sign attached to the fence that read *Brigadier Station*. Meghan straightened in her seat as the homestead appeared. Excitement curled in her stomach; it was just as she had imagined it would be. Set on higher ground with sloping views across the brown paddocks, the modest, cream coloured building had a veranda that wrapped around the front of the house, creating lots of comfortable nooks to take in the view.

Lachie parked the ute in a vacant spot in an old shed, next to a four-wheel drive and a tractor. As she climbed out of her seat, she wrinkled her nose as the aroma of hay and molasses wafted by. Familiar farm smells that brought back her earliest childhood memories. Meghan whirled around. Carefully pruned rose bushes stood proudly in the front garden beds. Strolling over to a bush burdened with white rose buds she touched the soft petals with her fingertips and inhaled their sweet fragrance.

"It's nice to see another woman appreciating my roses."

Startled, she looked over at the tall, older woman who had appeared by her side.

"I'm not much of a gardener, but I love flowers, roses in particular. I didn't think they grew out here."

"These are a hardy variety. My mother-in-law planted them before my time and showed me how to keep them going before she died. She was a cranky old lady, but she knew her stuff. She taught me a lot."

"Mum." Lachie bent down and hugged his mother with his free arm.

"Already giving Meghan gardening advice, I see."

Meghan offered her hand. "It's lovely to meet you, Mrs. McGuire."

Harriet's accepting hand was warm and soft. "Call me Harriet, honey. We're not formal out here."

Harriet McGuire had a face that looked like she laughed easily and often. Her shoulder-length hair was streaked with grey and had been cut by someone with a good eye for style. Behind her glasses were eyes just as blue as her son's. Harriet placed an arm around Meghan's back and led her inside.

"It'll be fun to have another woman in the house for a while. Gets a bit rowdy with two boys here."

"That wouldn't surprise me." Meghan grinned, touched by such a warm welcome.

Lachie dropped their bags haphazardly in the hallway before giving her a quick kiss.

"Just going to check the emails. Mum will help you settle in." Before either woman could object, he was disappearing down the hallway.

"He'll be busy for a while, I'm afraid." Harriet directed Meghan through the small but practical kitchen and into the larger living room.

"That's what happens when he takes time off. But I'm glad you could come back with him this time."

"I'm glad I could finally join him. Work has been so busy."

"Make yourself comfortable. I'll put the kettle on, then you can tell me all about yourself."

She slipped out of the room leaving Meghan to wander around the living room.

The inside of the house was every bit as welcoming as the outside. The walls were filled with photographs, and she took them all in, absorbing the family history. There were several black-and-white wedding photos and portraits of elegant men and women. She recognized Harriet in her wedding photo with her late husband. What had Lachie said his name was? David? No, Daniel. They were both attractive and looked good together.

The modern photos were all of the same three boys. A picture of them together caught her eye, and she studied it. The boys wore swimming shorts, and were sitting on a rock in a river, their hair wet. They looked similar with light brown hair and bright blue eyes. Meghan recognized Lachie and guessed him to be about ten in the photo.

Harriet reappeared and came to stand next to her.

"Those are the Brothers of Brigadier Station. They've been getting called that since they were little," she explained. "Did you recognize Lachie?"

Meghan nodded. "He's the oldest one."

"That's right. The one next to him is my youngest, Noah, he lives in New Zealand now. And that's Darcy." She pointed to the slim little boy in the picture, her voice softening. "He's still here. He's saving money to buy his own property one day."

"They all have your beautiful blue eyes."

"Yes, they are a good-looking bunch. Temperamental at times, but I'm proud of them. Lachie's had lots of responsibility put on him since Daniel died. He wasn't expecting to inherit Brigadier's until he was much older. Darcy has helped a lot with the workload which lets Lachie visit you in Townsville." Harriet smiled widely at her visitor. "Come, the jug's boiled."

Meghan followed her to the kitchen where she made cups of tea and set the table with freshly baked scones, strawberry jam, and cream.

"I hope you like it here."

"I love it so far. I can't wait to see more of the station."

Meghan topped her scone with jam and took a bite. It was still warm and melted in her mouth. "It's been a long time since I've had homemade scones and these are delicious."

"Thank you. I'm glad you like them."

Meghan was surprised to find out they had much in common despite the generational gap as they continued chatting. Harriet admitted to reading voraciously. "I like to support Australian writers in particular."

"Me too." Meghan sipped her tea. She found it comforting that Harriet, a woman born and raised in the country, would be an avid reader.

"Do your parents live in Townsville too?"

Meghan's shoulders slumped slightly. "My Dad died before I started school and Mum passed away in a car accident two years ago."

Harriet's voice softened. "I'm so sorry for your loss."

"Thank you. They were great people, and I miss them so much. Especially Mum, we were very close."

Tears threatened as they always did when talking about her family, but she pushed them back.

"Mum would have liked you."

"I'm sure I would have liked her too." Harriet sipped her tea. "Do have any other family? Brothers or sisters?"

"No, Mum never remarried. She was happy with her teaching career. She taught at one of the Catholic schools in Townsville. I have a best friend, Jodie, she's like family."

As they finished off their tea, the phone rang, and Harriet glanced at it. "I'll get the phone. When you're ready, you can go and unpack."

Downing the last of her black tea, a drink she would have to get used to as no one else drank coffee, Meghan collected her bags and went in search of Lachie's bedroom. All the bedrooms came off the same long hallway, and Lachie's appeared the first on her right. She knew it was his by the familiar, dirty clothes scattered on the floor. Obviously, Harriet didn't pick up after him. Meghan smiled; she'd given up the hope he would start being tidier.

His room was large, taken up by a king-size bed and matching dresser. Meghan put her bag on the bed and considered changing out of her jeans and T-shirt.

But, curiosity got the better of her, and she left the room and wandered further down the hall. She found two more bedrooms similar to Lachie's but without the mess; the bathroom, and a separate toilet. The large room at the end she presumed was Harriet's. A glance in told her she was right and, to her relief, she noticed an en-suite. At least she would only have to share a bathroom with Lachie and his brother.

After finding cupboards and the laundry, Meghan came to the office where Lachie sat, his chin resting in his palm as he scrutinized something on the computer screen.

"Hey, sexy," she purred as she came around to stand behind him and snuggled her head against his shoulder.

"Having fun?" He turned his head and kissed her cheek.

"Your Mum is on the phone. I found your room and put my bag in there. I presume we're sleeping together?"

"Yeah, Mum's cool with that. Do you want to see the horses?"

"Absolutely I do. You know I love horses."

"There's a path from the kitchen. Easy to find, past the chickens."

"You don't want to show me?"

He barely raised his eyes from the screen. "I'm sorry. I've got so much work to do."

Disappointed, but excited to explore, she took off in the direction he had said.

The dirt path stretched beside a row of young coolabah trees, past the chicken coop and down to a wooden stable. Meghan spotted a chestnut horse's head peeking out over a metal railing. Cautiously, she stretched out her hand so it could sniff her, then stroked its head gently when it appeared friendly. The long-forgotten smell of horse assailed her nostrils.

"Oh, aren't you a handsome boy! What's your name?" she cooed.

"Thank you for the compliment, but if you're talking to the horse, I don't know if she would appreciate being called handsome." The warm, masculine voice coming from behind the horse surprised her. She jumped back, lost her footing and landed butt first on the dirt floor. The stranger walked around and stopped abruptly when he saw her.

He must be the brother.

Heat filled her cheeks as she pushed herself back to standing and wiped at the back of her pants. She focused her gaze on his dirty jeans and the dark brown of his work boots. "I'm sorry, I didn't know you were in here."

"It's okay, I don't get to hear compliments that often." He sounded amused.

"I meant the horse," she stuttered. "S-she's beautiful."

"Yes, she is." His voice was soft.

Meghan tucked her hair behind her ear nervously, then looked up into his deep blue eyes. "Darcy, right?"

"And you must be Lachie's girlfriend." His easy smile produced a dimple on his unshaven cheek.

"Meghan." She tried to calm her pounding heart. What was wrong with her? Yes, he was ruggedly good looking, similar to Lachie but rougher and with a squarer jawline. Something about Darcy captured her gaze and refused to release it.

A small black and white dog appeared beside him and yelped for attention, breaking the moment.

"And who are you?" She smiled at the fox terrier.

"This is my dog, Joey. Go ahead he won't bite."

Bending down, she extended her hand for the dog to sniff. After a brief glance at his owner, the canine trotted over for a scratch.

She could feel Darcy watching her. She stood up and looked about the barn, but her eyes soon came back to rest on him.

Darcy shook his head, breaking the contact and pointed to a shelf behind her. "Can you hand me a brush, please?"

Meghan turned and surveyed an array of brushes, combs, and hoof picks before choosing one and handing it over, careful not to touch him. He nodded in thanks.

She turned her attention back to the mare. "She's a lovely horse."

He brushed the horse with long strokes. "This is Shadow. She's pregnant. Due in a week or so. That's why she's not in the paddock with the others."

Meghan stepped back. The mare's belly was

protruding, full with foal. She stroked it, and the baby inside rewarded her with a gentle kick against her hand.

"Do you ride?" He bent to brush the mare's legs, his denim clad buttocks caught her gaze.

She averted her eyes to a comb, grabbing it she began working on the horse's mane.

"I was born on a station near Charters Towers. My dad bred horses.

Mum used to say I was riding before I learnt how to walk." She smiled at the memory. "I remember sitting in front of my dad. He used to let me hold the reins."

"And you live in Townsville now?"

"Yep. Dad died when I was little, and we had to sell up and move."

Meghan remembered her early years on the station. Her mother and father still young and deeply in love, working side by side with the horses while she watched from a safe distance. A feeling of complete happiness and serenity enveloping her. Those years remained the happiest time of her life.

"I'm sorry to hear that. I know what it's like to lose a father," Darcy sympathized.

"It was a long time ago." After her father had died, her mother had mourned him for years. Meghan had struggled at school both academically and socially. The small unit they had moved to was claustrophobic, and the moist heat of summer was suffocating. Eventually, she had grown used to it, but the yearning for the country life had remained. Now, finally back on the land, she could almost feel the dust settling back into her veins.

Darcy's gravelly voice pulled her back to the present. "So, what do you think of Brigadier Station?"

"I haven't seen much of it yet. It's very dry and dusty."

"Yep. Queensland's dust bowl. We need a good wet season."

"I can imagine it's even more beautiful when it's green," she smiled, envisioning long green grass where cracked brown dirt lay shrivelling more every day.

"The drought will break someday," Darcy said surely. "Nothing lasts forever."

CHAPTER 3

*D*arcy watched Meghan with interest. She had a natural tenderness towards the mare. Her country upbringing was apparent in her confidence and ability as she expertly combed the horse's mane.

She was undoubtedly attractive, but instead of the blonde, high maintenance city girl with big boobs and little brains that were Lachie's usual choice, she was shorter and dark-haired. Tight blue jeans accentuated curvy hips. Memories of his ex-girlfriend briefly invaded his thoughts. He shook his head, ridding himself of unpleasant memories.

Darcy continued brushing his horse. His gaze frequently coming back to the woman beside him. Occasionally she would ask a question which he would answer with his usual honesty, but even when neither of them spoke there was a strange easiness between them.

"We should head back. Dinner's probably ready by now." He placed the tack back on the shelf and gestured for her to lead the way. She waited as he bolted the stable door in place behind them, keeping the mare safe inside.

"Thanks for letting me help. Please tell me if I get in your way," Meghan said as they walked side by side back to the house.

He turned to her, his mouth set in a straight line, his gaze steady on her. "I will. And just so you know, I never lie. Not to anyone." If there was one thing he hated, it was secrets and lies. He'd seen what damage they could cause, and was not about to repeat the sins of his father.

Meghan bit her bottom lip. As he studied the lines in her lips, he wondered about their softness.

Joey barked and ran up to the house. Darcy watched as his mother greeted the dog at the door.

"Come on. I smell dinner." They started walking back up the path.

Darcy couldn't imagine Meghan getting in his way. In fact, it might be nice to have a young woman around the place for a few days, especially if she could keep Lachie in line. God knows he needed it.

~

Meghan breathed in the cooler evening air and gazed across the brown plains. Lachie and Darcy were relaxing next to her in wicker chairs spaced out on the veranda specially to enjoy the evening sunsets. Both men had their long, denim-clad legs stretched out in front, a cold beer in hand.

Harriet came out and took the vacant seat closest to Meghan. A ready smile on her face.

"What work do you do in Townsville?"

"I'm a vet nurse at a surgery. We mainly see cats and dogs." Meghan sipped her beer, the crisp ale washing away her nerves.

"You must really love animals then." Harriet leaned towards her. The faint smell of perfume lingered, reminding Meghan of the similar scent her mother had worn.

"I've always loved animals. But it's hard work. I really only see sick or abandoned pets, which is hard." Even talking about it choked her up and she swallowed back the emotions. "I'd like to learn more about cattle and horses."

"You'll certainly get a chance to do that here."

Lachie leant forward to join the conversation. "She's also a great photographer, Mum. You should see her work."

Meghan felt her cheeks warm. "I love photography. Painting too, but only as a hobby."

"I'd love to see some of your work. I'm sure you're very talented." Harriet patted her hand lightly. The familiar action surprised Meghan. She had forgotten what it was like to be part of a family.

"I see you brought your camera with you," Harriet

nodded at the SLR on the coffee table. "Our sunsets are pretty spectacular."

"I'm always prepared."

"Speaking of." Darcy pointed to the huge orange disc hanging low in the Western sky. She snapped a continual stream of photos as the sun made its graceful descent below the horizon, streaking the sky red and orange for a few moments before darkness suddenly surrounded them.

"You don't see sunsets like that at home," Meghan breathed in awe as a cool breeze brushed her cheek.

"They are pretty spectacular," Darcy murmured.

"Come on then. I'm starving." Lachie's stomach growled in agreement.

Meghan collected her camera and followed the family inside to the dining room. She took the space next to Lachie while Darcy sat down opposite her.

Harriet's tender beef roast didn't disappoint. Meghan enjoyed every moist mouthful, unlike both the men who scoffed the meat and potatoes and picked at their greens.

"Seconds, Mum?" Lachie smiled sweetly.

Harriet nodded toward the bench. "There's plenty there. I cooked enough for sandwiches for the next few days too."

He stood and went to retrieve more.

"Do you ride any of the horses, Harriet?" Meghan asked, curious to see who Darcy had inherited his love of horses from.

"Not anymore. The horses are Darcy's. Lachie

doesn't like horses. He prefers his motorbike." Harriet turned her attention to Darcy. "You should take Meghan. Molly's a sweet, gentle horse for a beginner."

Darcy glanced at Harriet. "Her dad used to breed horses."

"Really?" Lachie returned to his seat with his plate loaded up. "I didn't know that."

Meghan brushed the comment off. "Yes, we had a small property near Charters Towers, but we sold it when Dad got sick. I haven't ridden much since."

Darcy shifted slightly in his seat. "I need to do a bore run tomorrow if you want to come."

"That would be great. Thanks." Meghan smiled, eager for the chance to ride and explore the vast station. "You don't mind, do you, Lachie?"

He shook his head in reply.

"Now, Meghan," Harriet patted her hand gently, "Lachie has brought a couple of girls' home in the past, I won't lie."

"More than the couple you know about," Darcy teased quietly. His mother shushed him and continued. "He usually likes blondes."

"Mum!" Lachie protested.

"It's true. Darcy's the one who likes brunettes."

Meghan glanced across the table at Darcy. His sun-kissed skin had a touch of pink on it, but he avoided her gaze.

"Anyway, it's lovely to have you here, for the next couple of weeks." Harriet raised her wine glass in a toast.

"While we're toasting then, I should tell you that Meghan and I are engaged," Lachie announced.

Meghan's eyes widened. She had almost forgotten the reason for their trip. Her pulse raced as she took in the reactions. Darcy's eyebrows were raised in disbelief.

"Congratulations!" Harriet cried out, clapping her hands together.

Meghan stood to accept a warm hug, relief sweeping through her.

"I never thought this day would come!"

Darcy shook his brother's hand with a forced smile plastered on his face.

Lachie didn't seem to notice. He had a smug smile and a cheeky twinkle in his eye.

Darcy turned to her, his voice light with humour. "Sure you want to join this family? He's a handful." Darcy nodded at Lachie.

Meghan grinned. "I think I can handle it."

Harriet clapped her hands together. "We should be celebrating with champagne or something bubbly. I don't have anything, though."

"Beer will do." Darcy raised his bottle. "To the happy couple."

"To the happy couple." Harriet cheered as they all clinked their drinks together.

As the others sat down, Darcy pushed his chair in and gathered his plate.

"Where are you going?" Harriet asked.

"Gotta check on the horses." Meghan found Darcy's

attention focused on the plates in his hands. "I'll be back late, so I'll say goodnight."

"Okay then. Good night." Harriet waved him off.

Harriet and Lachie dismissed him as if this behaviour were normal for Darcy. Meghan frowned at his excuse. They had already closed the stable for the evening. Why did he need to check on the horses again? She watched as he put his dishes in the sink and slipped quietly out of the house and into the chilly night.

"What's the deal with Darcy?" Meghan asked Lachie later as they were getting ready for bed. "Does he have a girlfriend?"

"Nah. He did in high school, but she did a number on him, and he hasn't dated much since."

"What did she do?"

"Who knows?" Lachie shrugged. "Darcy doesn't tell people much; he keeps to himself."

Meghan frowned and wondered what had happened. Darcy was good looking and would surely have women fighting over him if he lived in town. Perhaps he hadn't found one willing to live so remotely yet. Or perhaps he was a romantic and was holding out for true love. She liked the idea of that.

He must get lonely, though. She knew loneliness well enough.

She looked back at her fiancé. Lachie, Harriet, and Darcy were her family now. She couldn't have hoped for a better welcome or a better family to marry into.

~

Meghan woke to find the bed empty and sunshine streaming through the curtains. She had hoped that Lachie would wake her so they could have breakfast together. After quickly dressing in a pair of jeans and a T-shirt she headed to the kitchen.

"Good morning. How did you sleep?" Harriet stood at the kitchen counter kneading dough; the smell of baking filled the room.

"Amazingly well, thanks. Must be the fresh air."

"Good. The boys have left already and don't know when they'll be back. Help yourself to cereal and toast, or I can cook bacon and eggs for you."

"No, you're busy, and cereal sounds great." Meghan fixed her breakfast and chatted to Harriet while she ate. It had been a long time since she had enjoyed the company of an older woman and she was surprised how comfortable it was.

"I try to do a bunch of baking once a week. Bread, biscuits, and cakes. The boys like sweets for smoko."

"How far away is the supermarket?" Meghan polished off her Weetbix.

"There are two in Julia Creek, which is forty minutes away. But I only buy essentials from them or have them brought out on the mail run." Harriet adjusted the temperature on the oven in preparation for the next tray of Anzac biscuits. "I go west to Cloncurry once a month and do a big shop there."

"Cloncurry? Isn't that another couple of hours' drive?"

Harriet nodded. "That's why it's only once a month."

Meghan thought of Jodie. This was why she had insisted on her friend trying out country living before making such a huge move. They took things for granted in the city. Want a coffee? Go to a café. Want food delivered? No problem. Not out here. If you didn't have something in the fridge you couldn't just run down to the corner shop. Living out here was a whole different lifestyle.

"Don't you get lonely?"

Harriet gave her a knowing smile. "No, I'm in the Queensland Country Women's Association, and we meet regularly and fundraise, do art and craft, that sort of thing. Darcy has his camp-drafting. Lachie has his friends at the pub. Or he did before meeting you." Harriet wiped her hands on her apron and surveyed the counter. "We all support and help each other here. It's one of the best things about living in the country. You have friends everywhere. Anyone can fit in as long as they want too."

Meghan washed up her bowl and put it away. Turning to Harriet her voice was hoarse with emotion. "Thank you. For such a warm welcome."

The strong, sugary smell of golden syrup enveloped her as Harriet put her arms around her. It held all the comfort of a mother's tender embrace. Meghan's eyes welled with unshed tears.

"This is your home now. Your family." The sincerity

on Harriet's face was almost Meghan's undoing. She swiped at her eyes as she was released.

After a deep breath, she turned back to her new friend. "What can I do to help?"

"Would you mind getting the eggs for me from the chicken coop?"

"Sure." Meghan was happy to be useful, despite having never retrieved eggs from a coop before. Harriet pointed out the scrap bucket near the sink. "Feed them that too, please. The path is behind the rainwater tank."

Meghan followed the dirt path toward the large green tank. Last night she had learnt the family stored rainwater for bathing and cleaning.

Beside it was a pen with two large grunting pigs inside. They didn't look particularly friendly rooting around in the ground, so Meghan kept walking, spotting the henhouse a few feet further ahead.

The multi-coloured fowl were pecking at the grass inside their large wire enclosure but looked up when they saw her approach. Meghan could feel their beady eyes fixed on her as she unlatched the door and entered, closing it behind her. She emptied the bucket of scraps on the ground, and the chickens flocked to the food clearing a path for her to move through. In the sheltered area, covered with slats of wood, she found individual boxes filled with straw. She collected each warm egg until she came upon a box that was still occupied by a ginger chook. Her feathers fluffed up, sharp curved beak ready to strike as its head twitched.

Meghan chewed on her lip wondering if she should try to remove it.

After a failed attempt at trying to scare the hen, it shrilled angrily back at her in irritation.

It was just a chicken, after all. Nothing she couldn't handle.

Slowly she reached out her hand to get under the hen, when, suddenly it flew at her. Distracted by the whirlwind of feathers, Meghan felt a sudden pain in her hand.

"Ouch!" Meghan jumped back against the wall. The offending chicken looked at her, its head twitching from side to side, daring her to try that again.

"Okay, you win this round," she conceded. "But I'll win the war. Just wait and see."

To her surprise, the chicken casually jumped down from her nest and strutted out to join her friends. Meghan exhaled in relief and collected the warm eggs before the hen changed her mind.

She fought the impulse to run back to the house after she locked the coop behind her. Looking around she was glad no one had witnessed the event.

"Well done," Harriet exclaimed when she saw the success. "Did any of them peck you?"

"Just the one." Meghan absentmindedly rubbed her hand.

"You've gotta show her who's boss." Harriet squeezed her arm reassuringly.

~

Darcy and Lachie arrived home just after one o'clock. Meghan's breath caught as she saw the pair for the first time that day. She couldn't help noticing how good they looked in their faded blue work shirts and worn jeans. It was the first time she had seen Lachie wearing a battered cowboy hat. It was pulled low on his head to protect him from the harsh burning sun. The whole effect of his appearance left her warm and tingling.

Lachie stopped long enough to kiss her cheek and whisper a good morning in her ear. His attention then focused on food. He was always hungry. She envied his metabolism.

The conversation over sandwiches was work focused and impersonal. Meghan tried to keep up but quickly lost interest in talk of machinery and fire breaks.

Lachie's phone rang and, throwing an apologetic smile her way, he answered it and walked off to his office. Harriet cleared up the dishes and disappeared back into the kitchen.

Meghan found herself alone with Darcy as they finished off their cups of tea. "Did you do anything exciting this morning?"

Darcy scratched his nose. "We repaired a fence. Thrilling stuff."

"Well, I collected eggs." She smiled proudly.

"Impressive. Did you get pecked?"

"Yes. Only by one."

"Congratulations. You've earned that ride." He

finished off his tea, put his hat back on and headed for the door. "Come on."

She scrambled out of her chair and followed him outside. Hastily pulling her boots on at the door as Joey watched her, his tail wagging excitedly.

Shadow, the pregnant mare greeted her with a snort and Meghan quickly patted her as she followed Darcy, jogging to keep up with his long-legged stride. Through the stables there was a paddock where two horses roamed contentedly, their tails swishing at flies. A stocky brown pony trotted over and nudged Darcy's hand searching for treats.

"This is Molly." Darcy rubbed the pony's nose. Her age was evident from the greying hairs around her nostrils. "She's a softie. Mum brings her apples and spoils her."

Meghan patted her lovingly and tickled her chin. Molly closed her eyes enjoying the attention.

"Come on, girls," Darcy said as he led the way to the tack room. Swiftly with dexterous fingers, he saddled and bridled the mare while Meghan watched and befriended the horse. "She's an old girl, but she still loves a gallop. Just hold on if you lose control and I'll help you," he reassured her.

Meghan placed her foot in the stirrup, grabbed the saddle and hoisted herself up. He watched but refrained from helping. Once settled in her seat he adjusted the straps, his arm brushing her denim-clad calf.

Darcy handed her the reins and led her back out to the paddock. "Stay here. I'll be back in a minute."

Alone with the horse, she shuffled in her seat and got used to the feel of the hard saddle beneath her. It smelled freshly oiled. She held the reins. Molly's ears twitched but she stood silently, waiting for her commands. When she felt more confident, Meghan gave Molly a gentle kick and encouraged her to walk forward. The horse readily agreed, her gait smooth and fluid.

Instinct took over as together they walked around in circles, gradually increasing speed to a trot. Meghan matched the gentle rhythm, rising and fallen in time to the horse's gait.

"You're a natural." Darcy trotted over on a shiny black horse.

"It feels good to be back in the saddle."

"This is for you," he handed her an Akubra.

"Thanks." The fawn felt was smooth and new under her fingers. She put the hat on and pulled it low. It was a perfect fit. "What do you think?"

"You look like a cowgirl." His eyes trailed over her jeans, close fitting t-shirt, and brown boots. "Not turning into a Buckle Bunny, are you?"

"A what?"

"Buckle Bunny. The girls with sparkly belt buckles and too much makeup."

"What's the point of makeup out here? It would melt off straight away." She shrugged and readjusted the hat, wondering briefly where he had found it.

Darcy led his mount out of the paddock, leaning from his seat to open the gate and again to close it after Molly had walked through.

"You look like you know what you're doing," he said, reclaiming her attention.

"It's all coming back to me now." She reached down and stroked Molly's warm neck fondly. "So where are we going?"

"We need to track the bore lines and make sure water can flow through for the cows."

"What's a bore line?"

"It's over here." He pointed toward a tree line where a shallow trench was filled with murky water. Cows grazed lazily nearby; one skinny cream heifer drank from the water.

Four kangaroos jumped out from the trees and scattered into the fields. "Did you see that?" she asked excitedly.

"There are heaps of roos out here. They can survive the worst drought no problem. You'll probably see emus and wild pigs along here too."

"I saw the pigs in the pen this morning." Meghan absently swatted a fly buzzing around her head.

"Wild sows. I caught them a few months ago. You can't eat wild pigs straight away, though, they have all sorts of worms. We have to feed them scraps for a few months before slaughtering. Mum wants them for Christmas."

"Do you hunt pigs regularly then?"

"If I know there's one around, especially if it's

attacking the cattle, then I'll hunt it. We trap them occasionally for meat."

Meghan raised her eyebrows. "That's very self-sufficient."

"We butcher our own beef too. Used to run merino sheep when Noah was here. Dad got rid of them when Noah left, though. Shame really, I do miss lamb chops in spring. They're too expensive to buy these days."

Lulled into a dreamy state by the swaying rhythm of Molly's gait, Meghan kept her eyes on Darcy's broad back as he rode ahead. His muscles rippled as he rode along the dirt track and over a cattle grid. He turned around in the saddle suddenly, as though he could feel her eyes studying him. She looked away quickly, feeling a warm blush on her cheeks.

She battled for something to say. "What are the animals eating? Since there's hardly any grass."

"Cottonseed. It's full of enough nutrients to keep them alive, but unfortunately, it doesn't fatten them up." He pointed out a large trailer in the middle of the field. "That's our cottonseed feeder. We only have to fill it up once a month or so and they eat out of it. Occasionally, we put out some molasses lick too. They have fun eating that sticky stuff," he said with a grin.

Molly strained against the bridle as they approached a large empty paddock.

"You can let her run if you want." Darcy gestured ahead.

Meghan grinned and with a little kick Molly started to trot. With a little more encouragement, she sped up.

Meghan revelled in the wind rushing past her. She glanced back to see Darcy's mount was also galloping and he was catching up. "Come on, girl," she urged Molly along.

Despite having a faster and younger mount, he stayed a meter or two behind her as they galloped across the flat field. At last, she could sense the horse tyre, so she reigned her in. Darcy pulled up beside her, slightly breathless.

"Enjoy that?" He met her gaze with a smile so warm and engaging that she tingled all over.

"That was exhilarating!" Meghan flung her head back and her hands wide.

"Once you know the lay of the land, you'll be able to take her out." Admiration glimmered in his eyes.

"That would be great. I'd like to help out as much as I can."

Heat waves shimmered around the vast nothingness before them. It was as though they were the only things foolish enough to brave the afternoon sun.

While they inspected the land, Darcy told her about the station, about his family and the history. For three generations, the McGuire family had lived and died on Brigadier Station, working through the tough times of floods, droughts and economic hardships.

"It was my great-grandfather who first settled here. He was a brigadier in World War One, he came here afterwards. People would refer to this place as the Brigadier's station. The name stuck. He became one of the most successful cattlemen of his generation." The fondness and gratitude softened his voice. "Brigadier Station is a testament to his pioneering spirit."

The long-forgotten methane smell of cattle greeted her at the same time Darcy pointed out a mob of cattle grazing hungrily. "Here are some of our weaners. We've only got about four hundred left here. The rest are on agistment."

Meghan noted their golden honey colour. "What breed are they?"

"Droughtmaster. That's a cross between Brahman and Shorthorn. They're the best suited up here and fetch decent prices when we ship them. We also run a breeding program."

"How big is Brigadier?"

"Sixty thousand acres. We're only going to cover a small portion today."

Meghan was impressed by the vastness. Lachie had hinted that it was big, but she had had no idea of the vast size. She gazed over the flat dry plains. The boundaries of her little world so extended, further than her eyes could see.

Suddenly Molly shied and reared up, snorting in alarm. Instinctively, Meghan squeezed her thighs and held on tightly. Darcy swung from his horse and quickly caught Molly's reigns, murmuring softly and stroking her reassuringly.

"Hey, are you alright?"

Her cheeks warmed as his gaze did a quick but thorough inspection. Worry lingered in his eyes.

"I'm fine. How's Molly?" She leaned forward in the saddle and stroked Molly's neck.

"She's okay. Must have smelt a snake." He looked to a clump of stubborn brush. "That's their likely hiding spot."

Fear shimmied down her back. "Snakes?"

"Don't worry, I won't let anything happen to you."

Darcy caught her gaze and, mesmerized by those piercing blue eyes, the fear was replaced by a warm heat. Her heart beat faster. Surely it was adrenalin from the snake incident.

He was first to break the connection. "You'd better get used to it if you're going to live here. We have our fair share of danger."

~

The horses carefully picked their way across uneven terrain, sheltered by huge coolabah trees. Occasionally, Darcy pointed out birds or other things he thought might be of interest to Meghan.

Beneath her hat, her thick ponytail swung across her shoulders. She looked fragile, like a porcelain doll he had seen in a shop once. But, out here she became another part of the environment, as at home on these plains as the rabbits and kangaroos.

He stared at the view and lost himself in the desolation that stretched ahead of him. It was so damn hot. Too hot for this time of year. It had to cool down. It had to rain. Sometime.

"You were surprised when Lachie announced our engagement." Meghan's voice was etched with worry.

Darcy thought for a moment, careful not to say anything offensive, but wanting to be honest. "I'm surprised any woman could get Lachie to commit."

She laughed. "You're kidding? It wasn't really that hard."

He recalled all-nighters at the pub watching out for his intoxicated brother who was usually found slobbering over the latest backpacker turned waitress.

"Lachie's always been a player. Or at least, he was. You've changed him. It's been so gradual I barely noticed."

"He was never like that around me. He's always been very committed."

Darcy arched his eyebrows in surprise. "How long have you two been together?"

"Eight months."

"That's a pretty quick engagement then. Especially since this is your first time here. Unless he's planning on moving to Townsville?" He couldn't imagine Lachie giving up his birthright.

"No, we'll live here on the station."

"How do you know you'll like it?"

"I just do." She shrugged. "I don't mind cities and Townsville only has 170,000 people so it's not really that big. Just large enough for good shopping, pubs, and live entertainment, but small enough to find a quiet space when the crowds get too much."

She turned her attention to the never-ending horizon. "But, when I see these dusty fields and gum trees it's like I'm coming home. I guess that doesn't make sense. But it's true."

Darcy knew that feeling well. Whenever he returned from a trip, he felt relieved, like he could breathe again. The dust was his oxygen; he needed it to survive.

"Country life is tough. We all work hard, even Mum. A tree change doesn't mean life slows down."

"I can see that."

He pushed back his hat and scowled at the land. "Some fellas get sick of looking at the same view every day. Being isolated on a station in the thick of a blazing summer can drive people crazy. It's not an easy life if you're not used to it."

The wistful expression on her face made him realise how long it had been since he'd had a conversation with a woman who wasn't related to him or someone else's wife. He really needed to get out more.

"I don't think I could ever get sick of this place." Her words were soft. He wondered if she realised she'd spoken aloud. For a smart woman, she seemed caught up in the romance of the outback. He hoped, for her sake and Lachie's, she was prepared for a hard slog. Especially if the drought went on much longer.

Darcy knew of city girls who moved to the area hoping to meet a wealthy, handsome station heir. Mostly they returned home disheartened. Sometimes leaving broken marriages in their wake. But Meghan seemed honest in her intentions.

Cockatoos squawked above them as he took the lead as the path narrowed and the homestead came into sight. He contemplated the future and what having Meghan living with them would mean. He would have a sister-in-law. Another person to help out around the house and the station. A reminder that he would never have a wife and a family of his own unless he put himself back out there. He sighed. He couldn't risk another heartbreak. Meghan might think she was tough enough. He hoped she proved that to be true. But she would be one in a million. He wasn't as lucky as his brother.

Meghan's beautiful face would remind him of that every day.

CHAPTER 4

*T*he warm water soothed her aching body as Meghan stood in the shower letting the water wash away the dirt. She watched the muddy remnants swirl and slip down the plughole, knowing she would be sore tomorrow.

She thought back to the ride with Darcy. He was protective of his older brother, asking her questions and checking on her motives. It must have been fun for them growing up. Having siblings to share their childhood with. Constant playmates to cause mischief with and forge lifelong bonds. She wished she could press re-wind to a time of childhood innocence. When there was no death, no drought. To the time her parents were still alive to hold her hand and tell her happy endings did exist.

She dressed in a simple short denim skirt and pink shirt. She was drying her hair with a towel in front of the mirror when Lachie appeared in the doorway.

"Did you go riding?" he asked as he lay down and spread out on the bed.

"Yeah, Darcy took me." She put down the towel and climbed onto the bed next to him. He looked tired and worn out. She curled up next to him, and he draped his arm over her shoulder.

"Busy day?"

"Very." He sighed. "I'm sorry I can't spend more time with you."

"That's okay. I loved looking around the station today. It's so beautiful."

Lachie murmured in agreement as she played with his shirt buttons.

"I think we should have the wedding here." She looked up to see his reaction.

"You want to?" He sounded surprised.

"Yeah, it makes sense. It will be such a small wedding anyway. Just your family and a few friends."

"Okay. When?"

"How long does it take to plan a wedding? A few weeks?" She tapped her finger to her lips, "I want to live here. I want our life to start. Now."

"Alright then. Better before the wet season starts. Then if we get cut off, we'll have each other to entertain." He rolled on top of her and kissed her neck. He obviously wasn't that tired after all.

"Dinner's ready," Harriet sang out from the other side of the closed bedroom door.

Lachie slumped disappointedly against Meghan, who couldn't help but giggle at the interruption.

"Thanks, Mum," Lachie called back when Harriet knocked on their door.

"Come on. Let's go tell her we've set a date."

~

"I always wanted to host a wedding here!" Harriet hugged her soon-to-be daughter-in-law excitedly when they told her their plans.

"It'll be nothing too fancy, and I'll take care of all the planning." Meghan didn't want to be a burden to Harriet, she was certainly busy enough running the household.

"Let me do something! The flowers and food? You don't want to bring everything up from Townsville."

Meghan could see it would mean a lot to her. "Okay, the food. But we don't need flowers. We can get married in front of the roses."

Harriett touched her hand over her heart, tears glistening in her eyes. "Oh, yes. That will be beautiful."

Darcy's tall, rugged figure appeared at the screen door. He stooped slightly, removing his dirty boots, before opening the door.

"Darcy." Harriet couldn't wait for the poor man to get inside before sharing the news. "The wedding's going to be here!" She was bubbling over with enthusiasm.

"Yeah?" Darcy glanced at Meghan and Lachie briefly. "Save me a trip to Townsville." He made his way to the sink and washed his hands. Lachie stood next to his brother and they chatted about cattle in the west paddock. Meghan watched their easy manner towards each other as they laughed and joked good-naturedly.

Lachie winked at her before turning back to his brother. "Darcy, be my best man?"

Darcy looked up in surprise before covering it with a joke. "I already am the best man." Lachie slapped him on the back affectionately. "Then why am I the one getting married first?" He grinned widely and walked away. Darcy's gaze fell on Meghan briefly, and she wondered again why he was still single.

It was the middle of the night when Meghan slipped out of bed to use the bathroom. She tiptoed down the hall in her white cotton singlet and pink shorts. The old house was quiet and peaceful.

She jumped backward as the bathroom door opened a few feet ahead of her and light spilt out, illuminating Darcy's tall frame. His bare shoulders filled the doorway.

"You okay?" He reached out to steady her arm.

She felt her blood warm as she considered the golden-toned flesh above a pair of black shorts. She had no idea such a toned body was hiding under his worn work clothes.

His own eyes were on her scantily-clad body. Nervously she crossed her arms across her chest. Her breath was coming quick now. "You didn't hang around after dinner."

He cleared his throat and looked back at her face. "No." He shook his head slightly as if trying to remember where he had been. "Shadow is close to foaling, and she showed some signs of it starting."

"Is she okay?"

"She's fine. False alarm." He moved sideways so she could pass.

As she moved closer, she could smell the familiar combination of horse and hay. It made her stop and breathe it in.

She turned slightly and found herself inches away from his solid chest.

"Darcy, will you come get me if Shadow goes into labour? I'd like to be there. To help if I can."

He raised his arm and rubbed his neck. "She'll do all the hard work, but if you're still here, I'll get you."

"Thank you. It interests me. As a vet nurse, I mean."

She was about to move when she spotted a jagged scar over his heart. Without thinking, she touched it. "How did you get this?" Under her fingers, she could feel his heart thumping. His chest rose as he took a sharp breath. She raised her eyes and got distracted looking at his mouth.

He licked his dry lips before backing away from her. "That's a story for another day." He slipped into his room and closed the door firmly behind him.

～

Darcy leaned back against the wooden barrier. Right now it was the only thing stopping him from taking that soft, supple body in his arms. Her fruity scent still lingered in his nostrils. He glanced at his bed and imagined her on it. Her soft pale skin under his hands, her lips under his. He flexed his hands trying to rid them of the need to touch her.Her barely clad presence had left little to the imagination. Her perky breasts with their dark pointy tips made him realise the full extent of his desire for her. There was no use pretending he wasn't madly attracted to her and sometimes when she looked back at him he wondered if she felt the same. That kind of chemistry was hard to dismiss.

But what was the point in that? He was a fool to think that way about her – his brother's fiancé.

The most he could hope for was friendship. He had to stay strong and avoid any physical contact. Perhaps he could slake his desire with another woman in town one night. Maybe, he could find a backpacker or tourist just passing through who would be happy enough to share his swag for a night. He didn't need any kind of long-term complications.

He slipped into bed hoping he could switch off and not think about the beauty next door, in bed with his brother.

CHAPTER 5

The next day Harriet drove Meghan to their neighbour's station. The homestead was similar to the one at Brigadier's—low set with deep shady verandas surrounded with shade trees. The dehydrated paddocks surrounding it were empty except for the occasional whisper of brown dust.

Maddie Sears welcomed her with a friendly hug. Her smile was genuine and honest. This was a woman who could become a good friend, despite being a few years older than Meghan. Like most outback women, Maddie wore her auburn hair long and tied back, her sun-bronzed face was etched with faint worry lines.

"What do you think of the country?" Maddie asked as she poured hot tea into mugs.

"It's bigger than I expected," Meghan replied accepting her cup. "There's a vastness I hadn't expected."

Maddie smiled knowingly. "I think you either love

country life, or you hate it. I love it. But I'm from Mount Isa, so this is all I know."

Harriet nodded in agreement. "Well, she better love it because Meghan and Lachie are engaged."

A squeal escaped Maddie's open mouth. "Congratulations. He's a catch."

"Thank you." Heat crept up her neck. "Why is everyone so shocked by this news?"

Maddie glanced at Harriet who shrugged. "Lachie has a reputation as a ladies' man."

"Obviously, he's grown out of it now," Harriet assured her with a gentle pat on the knee.

"Anyway, I moved here three years ago, when I married Dylan. So, if you have any questions, ask me. Everyone is really friendly and welcoming." Maddie had an earthy wholesomeness about her, like Harriet. As though they had become part of their environment. A strange sense of satisfaction filtered through Meghan.

"Thanks, I will." She sipped her tea as the conversation turned to other topics.

"Is Darcy competing this weekend?" Maddie asked Harriet. "Everyone loves watching Darcy on that horse of his."

Harriet smiled proudly. "He is. He's pretty confident for this round, and Jasper is in top nick. Are you bringing the children?"

"I'm not sure. Jamie's a little young for such a rowdy weekend."

A pretty woman in her early twenties with a long

blonde ponytail popped her head around the living room door. "Excuse me?"

"Briar, come meet Lachie's fiancé." Maddie encouraged. "Meghan, this is our Guvvie Briar."

The younger woman raised her eyebrows. "Lachie's getting married. Well done."

"Thanks. Excuse my ignorance, but what's a Guvvie?" Meghan asked curiously.

"Governess. I look after the kids," she explained.

"Briar is a godsend! Dylan has an eight-year-old daughter from his first marriage, and she does School of the Air. Briar helps her with that and generally helps with the kids."

"School of the Air?"

"The Julia Creek School is forty minutes away. School of the Air is done online." Maddie explained.

"Back before the internet, my boys did it over the radio and through the post. It's much easier now," Harriet said.

"Wow." The extent of the workload for a woman in the outback was enormous, not only did they cook, clean, run a household, home-school their kids, grow their own vegetables and raise livestock, but they were also expected to help out on the station too. Darcy was right, it's not a quiet life. She could certainly see why Guvvies were useful.

"Emma's finished her work, and I'd like to take her swimming if that's alright?" Briar asked Maddie.

"Sounds like a good idea. Thanks."

Meghan watched the younger woman slip away.

Today felt like a preview of what her life would be. Maddie was the ultimate country wife and played the role well. Like Harriet she didn't complain or moan, she simply did the best she could. Having such strong, confident women around would be a help for her as she found her way in this new life. Meghan was grateful. She wondered how many other newcomers would receive such support.

The soft moans of a crying baby had Maddie on her feet. "I'll just get Jamie, he'll be after a feed." She walked off down the hall.

Harriet leant in close to Meghan. "Maddie and Dylan run sheep as well as cattle. Although, they sold most of their cattle last year. The drought has hit them pretty hard, and they are only just scraping by."

Meghan pressed her hand to her heart. She had never had to endure such hardship. She could only imagine how tough these families were doing it. How much they must struggle just to put food on the table. "Are many stations selling their stock?"

"Most have already sold all they can or keep them on agistment. We've seen a few stations sold or abandoned. One lot even sold to a Chinese buyer."

"Will that affect the area?"

"Who knows. No one else wanted to buy the station though. I'm sure they would have preferred to sell to Australians."

Maddie returned with her nappy-clad son on her hip. His thick, black hair was tousled from his sleep.

Meghan gazed upon his chubby face and big brown eyes. "He's gorgeous. How old is he?"

"Seven months," Maddie sat her son on the floor surrounded by toys, "He's a blessing. I was told I couldn't have kids, and then, surprise! I got pregnant."

"Wow," Meghan replied, entranced by the small child as she watched him chew on a toy giraffe. She timidly stroked his soft, silky cheek. His eyes found hers, and she felt a fluttering in her chest.

Having grown up without any siblings or cousins, Meghan's experience was limited to the kids she had occasionally babysat in her teen years. Babies were entirely new to her, and she watched every gurgle and smile with wonder. This little baby boy was simply the most adorable creature she had ever seen. When he wrapped his fingers around hers, a physical ache settled in her stomach. Suddenly she knew, without a doubt, she wanted a baby of her own one day. The thought of being able to raise her children on Brigadier Station, surrounded by family and friends, with animals to raise, horses and motorbikes to ride, sounded like a dream. Emotion ached in her throat. She only wished her mother was still alive so she could be there for her future grandchildren. Harriet would be a wonderful grandmother. The children would never want for love, there would be so many people showering it over them.

She realised it might be a full, busy life for the wives out here, but it was also rewarding in many ways. She would never be able to live in the city again after this.

Traffic, strangers, pollution. That all seemed a lifetime ago. Her past. This was where her future lay. Brigadier Station was her future.

～

The following days flew by. Meghan spent most of her time following Harriet around helping with housework and cooking. They had become easy friends and Meghan came to admire her future mother-in-law. Harriet was an independent countrywoman used to doing it tough, and yet she was also generous with her praise and smiles. Meghan was enjoying their closeness, but saw a flicker cross her friend's face every now and again. Especially when Lachie's father, Daniel was brought up in conversation, which wasn't often. Meghan knew how painful the unexpected loss of a loved one could be, and to lose a beloved husband must have been heartbreaking. Meghan tried to show her empathy, but Harriet preferred to avoid the subject. It seemed that Daniel's passing was still raw and painful to discuss.

As well as collecting eggs and feeding the chooks each day, Meghan also took on the job of feeding the pigs and cattle kept in the home paddock. She took great joy in watching the mother cow with her calf and the three orphaned calves she had adopted.

"We usually end up with a few poddy calves each season," Lachie had explained. Meghan couldn't wait for spring when she could hand raise a calf herself. She daydreamed about using formula in a bottle and hand-feeding the little orphans and becoming lifelong friends. She had hand reared kittens and puppies in the same way. Even the occasional rescued joey kangaroo had been brought in for temporary foster caring at the clinic.

She worked tirelessly in the large veggie patch planting tomatoes, lettuces, and herbs. "Is there anything else we can grow?" she asked Harriet who shook her head.

"We can only grow crops over winter. By October, it's too damn hot, and everything dies. It's a pain because fruit and veggies cost a fortune and they're mostly old and overripe by the time we get them. That's why we eat so much canned and frozen food."

Meghan took particular note of the meals cooked. Plenty of proteins and carbohydrates. Potatoes, rice or pasta, accompanied every meal, including breakfast which was a spectacular feast of bacon, sausages, scrambled eggs, mushrooms, baked beans and hash browns. It could keep the men going until dinner if necessary. Sometimes they would take sandwiches with them if they were working away, but sometimes they would forget to eat lunch and come home, stomachs rumbling late after dark.

She regularly found herself wandering to the horse yard in her spare time. It was Darcy's domain. He owned and cared for the horses. Sometimes she would find him there and he would let her help feed and brush them. Their conversation always light and friendly.

Molly especially enjoyed Meghan's visits. She often took the horses apples or other treats. Molly would crunch and slobber juice, her eyes closed in equine ecstasy.

Shadow would always get lots of scratches at the spot around her ears Meghan knew she loved.

This afternoon she found Darcy practicing his campdrafting skills with Jasper. The horse concentrating every bit as hard as his rider as he turned sharply around barrels, kicking up dust in his wake.

His brown Akubra shading his eyes from the low sun, Darcy rode over to the railing where she stood watching with Joey obediently at her side.

"What's campdrafting all about?" She stroked Jasper's nose.

"Well, the rider and his horse, cut a beast from a mob. Then directs the animal around a figure eight and then through a set of gates. He's assigned points based on technique and time." His voice was filled with infectious passion. She noticed that sometimes, in unguarded moments he let his true feelings show.

Nodding with understanding, Meghan tried to imagine it. "How often do you compete?"

"I only compete locally at Julia Creek and Richmond. Sometimes Hughenden. I used to do the whole circuit before Dad died, now I don't have the time, and it's pretty expensive."

"Do you ever win?"

"Sometimes. It depends on who else is competing." He lifted his hat and wiped sweat from his brow with the sleeve of his work shirt.

"Are there any competitions coming up soon?"

"Julia Creek campdraft is this weekend. Didn't Lachie tell you?"

"No, he didn't. Oh, that's what Harriet and Maddie were talking about." She recalled their conversation.

"It's a big social event round here."

Meghan chewed on the inside of her cheek. When it came to socialising, her anxiety rose. She had a habit of keeping to herself. Jodie was the outgoing one. Being friends with her meant Meghan could hide in the shadows and wait until her trust had been earned.

"Okay, I'll come." She grinned. "If you tell me how you got that scar." She remembered the jagged line on his chest and her stomach clenched as visions of him, half naked returned from her memory.

The smile faded, and his eyes clouded. She saw the vulnerability he kept so well hidden. "Just an occupational hazard when you work with cattle. Dad had a busted knee after being knocked over by a bull."

She could gauge his expression. Honesty was as much a part of him as his well-worn Akubra. He didn't want to concern her with his medical history. No doubt this wasn't the only scar on his body. Lachie had plenty. War wounds he called them.

Jasper tossed his head, snatching at the bit. Darcy leant over and murmured in his ear while stroking his neck.

An unfamiliar restlessness tugged within her. Darcy shared a special relationship with his horse. He trusted Jasper with his life. Meghan didn't trust anyone that way. She loved Jodie and Lachie. But she didn't share everything with them. Not many people could be trusted that way.

CHAPTER 6

*T*he Julia Creek Campdraft was an annual event that pulled crowds from near and far. When they arrived, McIntyre Park was already jam-packed with enthusiastic spectators decked out in their best western-style shirts, boots and wide brimmed hats.

Meghan readjusted her Akubra as she watched Lachie and Darcy set up a makeshift yard for Darcy's horse, Jasper.

Harriet took Meghan's hand. "Come, I'll show you around and introduce you to some people." Meghan followed her gratefully. She hated feeling unnecessary while people had work to do.

The women made their way past makeshift camp-sites where families and friends huddled on picnic blankets or on the backs of trucks that had been parked there since before sunrise. Meghan gazed admiringly at the stockmen, graziers, ringers, station hands and their partners. They had taken the time out from their busy lives, burdened by the never-ending drought, to come, possibly hundreds of kilometres to this event.

She pulled her Akubra lower, feeling like a phony in her blue jeans, purple blouse and dirty boots. She had purposely avoided any type of sparkly belt buckle, and grinned when she saw two tall blonde girls pass her. Their glitzy buckles threaded through too-tight denim jeans.

Harriet stopped more frequently to chat to people as they approach the circling grandstands. After fifty-five years in the district, both at Brigadier Station, and before that on her father's property, she knew all the locals and event regulars. Everyone greeted Harriet McGuire with respect and admiration. In turn, she proudly introduced her friends to her soon-to-be daughter-in-law.

"Congratulations. Lachlan is finally settling down!" one woman gushed. "He and my daughter, Eve, went out for a few months' years ago. I had wondered if they would tie the knot. But now she's married with two littlies and lives up north."

Darcy was right about his brother. Lachie had dated most of the girls from local stations. Nothing serious and there were no hard feelings, but it seemed he did have a reputation as a player.

"Is Lachie the only heartbreaker in the family? What about Noah and Darcy?" she asked Harriet as they walked along.

"Noah has been with Jade since he left school and

most of that time they've been in New Zealand. Darcy has had a couple of girlfriends, but no one stuck. I hope he meets someone one day."

"He's handsome enough. I thought girls would be lining up."

"Not anymore. Now we better head to the arena. Darcy's round will be starting soon."

Harriet and Meghan found spots leaning against the wooden rails of the fence so they could have the best view. Lachie joined them, and they watched as one at a time a stockman on a horse would cut a beast from a small herd then they had forty seconds to manoeuvre it around a figure eight and get it through the gate.

"They get marked on the best control of the beast, riding skills, speed and being able to complete the course in time," Harriet pointed out the obstacles. "They have to show the horse's speed and agility. Darcy spends hours on Jasper training him specifically for campdrafting."

"Is it dangerous?" Meghan rested her head against her hand.

"Not if you know what you're doing." Lachie shuffled beside her.

"Next competitor is Darcy McGuire from Brigadier Station," The MC announced over the crackling speaker. Entranced by his easy grace and fluid motions, Meghan watched Darcy mount his horse and enter the ring. Attentively he stalked the mob observing which cow would give him the best resistance. With a beast chosen, he moved as an extension of his horse steering

Jasper to show their ability. Once through the first gate, Darcy never lost control of the cow and skilfully directed it around the course. Meghan joined the cheering crowd as he moved it through the final gate in near record time. Graciously, he tipped his hat in appreciation, his eyes locking on Meghan's. Her breath caught in her throat transfixed by his attention. He smiled proudly before leading his horse out.

"He'll be through to the second round for sure," Lachie's warm breath was at her ear, pulling her from her reverie. "That cow was never getting away."

"I'm surprised you're not in there," she nudged him teasingly.

"I'm not a big fan of horses to be honest. I prefer power over horse power."

"Noah used to campdraft with Darcy," Harriet offered. "They were so competitive. He likes his rodeos now. Apparently, he's quite good on the bucking horses."

"You must miss him. Do you see him often?" Meghan wondered about the elusive third son.

"No, unfortunately. He came back briefly when Daniel died but not again since. I keep meaning to plan a trip, but I don't even have a passport."

"Maybe he'll come for the wedding," Meghan suggested hopefully. Harriet shrugged.

Again, Lachie leant in so his mother wouldn't hear him. "Don't get your hopes up. Noah and I don't get on too well. Childish argument he hasn't gotten over. Besides, he likes his sheep in Otago now."

Meghan raised her eyebrows and was about to ask for more information when, from the corner of her eye, she saw Darcy approaching.

Water bottle in hand, he strode purposefully toward them.

"Congratulations, darling." Harriet hugged him. "That was a great ride."

"Thanks Mum." He returned the brief embrace.

"Excuse me, I have CWA business to attend to." Harriet winked and walked away.

"Well done, Mate." Lachie slapped Darcy's shoulder briefly. "Now, I need to talk to a man about a truck." He lifted a hand in a wave and scurried off.

Meghan sighed as Lachie disappeared into the crowd. He was starting to make a habit of leaving her on her own.

Darcy placed a hand on her arm. "He's serious. We need a new truck, and that would bore you to death."

She smiled and turned her focus back to Darcy, conscious of the heat radiating on her skin where he had touched her. "Your riding was incredible. Well done."

"Thanks. I almost lost it at one point, but Jasper pulled it back."

"Well, if it helps I didn't notice that. You were amazing." Her face grew hot as she stumbled over her words. "You make it look really effortless."

"Thanks," he smiled back, his eyes crinkling at the edges. "Want a burger?"

In response, her stomach growled loudly. It was hours since they'd eaten.

"Yes, please."

Darcy led the way to the barbeques that were sending delicious aroma of beef steaks, sausages and onions into the air.

"Two steak burgers and cokes," Darcy ordered and paid before she could reach for her wallet.

"Best steak burgers in Queensland," he said, digging his hand in his pockets and leaning against the table.

Meghan fidgeted with the hem of her shirt, suddenly nervous in his presence. "How long have you been campdrafting?"

"I was eight when I started competing." The burgers and drinks were handed over, and they found an empty table nearby to eat at.

"Eight is a bit young, isn't it?"

"I'd already been riding for a while by then. I'll stop when I don't enjoy it anymore." He bit into his burger, barbeque sauce dripping down his fingers.

Self-consciously, Meghan wiped at her face between bites with a serviette. "So, it's a big sport?"

"After racing, it's the biggest horse sport in Australia. It's even getting popular in America."

"What do you get if you win?"

"The payouts are pretty good, especially in the bigger competitions down south. But it's an expensive sport. Cost of entry fees, horse floats, vet bills, tack and equipment all add up. Not to mention the time I have to spend training and away from the station."

This was Darcy's passion – she could see it in his eyes. He belonged on horseback, working with these animals. This is what made him happy.

~

It was rare that everything went well in the arena. You never knew what attitude or temperament the beasts were in, and you didn't get much time to choose which one to push through. Darcy watched his fellow competitors cut grumpy bovines who seemed to know all the tricks. Time and time again the judge cracked the whip on them, indicating they were disqualified.

Luck was on his side today. Darcy made it through his second run with another high score. He wasn't in the lead, but anything could happen. He would have to wait to hear if he made it into the final round tonight.

In the meantime, he was keeping Meghan company. She seemed happy to stay at his side and watch the action from the stands. She asked lots of intelligent questions and that shouldn't have surprised him. She was a vet nurse so she knew a fair amount about animals and their instincts.

"Campdrafting horses have to have natural instincts. They have to want to do this. Breeding is important but it's also a lot of hard work. I've been training Jasper since he was a foal. I broke him and have trained him almost every day since," he said.

"No wonder you don't have a girlfriend – you're in

love with your horse." Her cheeky grin pulled him from his serious thoughts.

"Jasper is very loyal and devoted to me. What more could a guy want?" He joked back.

Meghan motioned to the people around them. "Seriously, why don't you date? There are still plenty of single girls here."

Darcy looked at the familiar women around them. Lachie had dated most of them at some point or another. So, even if he was looking to meet a woman he wasn't sure he wanted to be compared to his older brother.

"Nah," he turned his gaze blankly to the centre ring. "All the good ones are taken by now."

She nudged him with her shoulder. "Careful. You'll turn into the guy version of a crazy cat lady."

"I prefer dogs," he quipped back with a playful grin.

The atmosphere was electric, the anticipation high, as the final riders competed. They were all good, and it was hard for Meghan to understand why some riders got higher points than others. She may be prejudiced, but Darcy was the best rider she had seen all day and Jasper was the most amazing horse she had ever seen in action.

The pair leaned against the cold metal of the holding pens waiting for the results to be tallied. Anticipation flooded through her while Darcy stood casually composed beside her. Occasionally, people would approach to congratulate him on his first two rides. Politely he would thank them and introduce Meghan to his various friends and neighbours.

Finally, the results were announced and Darcy's shoulders sagged in relief as his name was called.

"Yes!" she hooted, and jumped up and down. "I knew you'd make it."

A slow grin tugged at the corner of his mouth and his eyes crinkled at the corners setting her heart rate fluttering. "Glad you were certain. I didn't think I had a hope in hell."

"Seriously? You were a shoe-in. I won't be surprised if you win today."

Her excitement was palpable as they went back to Jasper's holding paddock and readied him for the final draft. Meghan stroked his neck and congratulated the horse on his previous performances. "One more ride, Jasper. You got this." She ran her fingers over his black mane which was cut short, about two inches long, and it spiked against her fingers. The smells of dust and horse feed lingered.

After saddling Jasper up, they returned to the waiting bay. It wasn't long before it was Darcy's turn. Meghan stretched up on her tiptoes and kissed his cheek. "Good luck."

Darcy responded with a smile as butterflies fluttered in her stomach.

He launched himself easily into the saddle. Turning to her he winked. "Don't forget your camera."

She held it up showing she was prepared. Maybe Harriet would frame a photo if she took one good enough. It could go up on the wall in the living room. She would feel like a true part of the family then.

Meghan returned to the stands and found a spot with a good view point of Darcy. Through her camera lens, she took a continuous stream of photos.

Darcy had selected a stubborner cow this time, and it took longer to get him through the first gate. On the obstacle course, he and Jasper controlled the animal skilfully, and the crowd roared when he finished with another high score.

As Darcy was waving to the crowd, Lachie sidled up beside her.

"How'd he go?"

She smelt the strong odour of lager on his breath as his words slurred. "You didn't watch?"

"Was busy catching up with some mates." He put his arms around Meghan's waist and nibbled at her neck. "Fancy a shag in my swag?"

Meghan squirmed out of his hold. "No. You're drunk. Besides, I want to see if Darcy wins."

"Your loss." He said with a shrug.

Meghan watched him stumble away. What had come over him? In Townsville he was always attentive to her and rarely left her side. Here, in a completely new environment, he barely paid her any attention at all. Leaving his mother and brother to entertain her.

This was his stomping ground though, childhood friends and acquaintances he rarely saw. Of course, he would want to spend time with them and catch up on their news. Besides, she was in safe hands with Darcy. She was certainly enjoying herself more than if she was following Lachie around like a love-sick puppy. She had plenty to talk about with Darcy and they had reached a comfortable friendship. She was going to spend the rest of her life with Lachie, she would let him have a night out with his friends. She didn't want to be one of those wives who expected her husband to be by her side every night.

The announcement finally crackled through the speaker. Novice placings first, followed by the women's round. Then the one she was waiting for.

"Second place goes to Darcy McGuire." The gruff voice announced.

Meghan clapped loudly, disappointed Darcy hadn't won, but knowing he had tried hard and been up against some stiff competition. As he came out to receive his award, she snapped some photos. He waved to the crowd and smiled proudly at her. She lowered her camera and waved back, her eyes locked on his.

Darcy was pleased with his performance but relieved when it was over. He realised he was more nervous than usual knowing Meghan was in the audience. However, her support had made him more determined to do his best and Jasper had followed his lead perfectly.

From his vantage point in the stockyard, he had watched his brother stumble drunkenly through the crowd and talk to Meghan. He had hoped Lachie would behave with her here, but instead he did what he normally did at these social opportunities and used the chance to get drunk and act uncouth.

Darcy felt bad for her. This was all new to her and he wanted her to enjoy this event. It was always a highlight of the year for him. The atmosphere, the people, the music. He wanted to share it with her even if his brother didn't.

She hurried through the crowd and when she reached him, he was rewarded with her slight body pressed against his in a hug. "Well done."

He wrapped his arms around her and breathed in her scent. Dust and horses and Meghan. A combination he found surprisingly alluring. Lachie didn't deserve this lovely woman.

Finally pulling away she looked up at him, "What will you do with your winnings?"

"It'll go towards buying my own property someday." A property where he was the boss and could do what he wanted. "Did you see Mum?"

Meghan scanned the crowd. "She was sitting with her friends. She'll be thrilled for you."

Together they washed and fed Jasper and settled him in for the night in the temporary yard next to their makeshift camp site. Darcy led the way to the noisy gathering which had formed near the canteen. Harriet waved to them from her chair, surrounded by her sister Beverly and other friends.

"Well done, Darcy, good job." She hugged him. "I'm so proud of you."

"Thanks, Mum." He smiled back. She was his biggest fan and he knew she would have been watching intently. She turned to Meghan. "I saw you in the stands enjoying yourself so I left you to it."

"I took lots of photos. Hopefully there are some good ones of Darcy."

Darcy spotted a couple of foldout chairs, and he pulled one out and offered it to Meghan before placing the other beside her. Harriet offered them both a cold drink from a cooler next to her filled with drinks and snacks. The older ladies were gossiping, and Meghan couldn't follow along so Darcy, who was subjected to being his mother's sounding board, whispered the gossip so only Meghan could hear.

"Caroline moved back in with her parents..." Harriet said.

"Because her husband came home and found her in bed with a drover." Darcy whispered. "Now the husband has shacked up with the teacher."

"It's better than daytime TV." Meghan laughed.

"Gossipy lot here. Can't help knowing each other's business, though."

The band started playing, and Darcy spotted some friends he knew. He introduced Megan to the men, who consisted mostly of graziers' sons. Over the buffet dinner, stories were told of other campdrafts and incidents that had occurred. The guys especially loved sharing Darcy's embarrassing moments in the ring.

"One of his first competitions he got this rough calf, and his horse was still pretty green. Anyway, it ended up throwing him and he landed hard on his arm."

"Bloody well broke my arm." Darcy's strong country accent seemed more pronounced. "The devil was in that cow, I tell you."

After the meal and a few drinks, the crowd got livelier, and people started dancing. Meghan got pulled up when Darcy was getting another round. He watched her dance animatedly to Lee Kernigan. She glanced back at him every so often and pulled faces. The shy girl was stripped away and replaced by a confident, beautiful woman.

Finally, Darcy and the other guys joined them, and they all danced around singing along to songs by Brooks and Dunn and Alan Jackson at the top of their voices.

The floor emptied as a popular ballad started. With his heart in his throat, Darcy offered her his hands for a slow dance. Without hesitation, she stepped into his arms, placing a hand on his shoulder, the other fitting in his large palm. Their faces were mere centimetres apart as they swayed back and forth. As the song played their bodies moved closer and she rested her head on his chest. He breathed in her floral scent. Damn, it had been a long time since he'd held a woman. And what a woman she was with her petite frame and soft curves. His fingers started lazily stroking the small of her back. She squeezed his hand lightly, and he replied by rubbing his thumb over hers. As the song came to a close they broke apart.

"Feel like a change of scenery?" Darcy asked, slipping his hands in his pockets.

She nodded in reply, her lips tight as though she didn't trust herself to speak.

~

Darcy found himself unexpectedly cold after having Meghan's warm body against him. It had felt so natural and easy. Their bodies fitted together perfectly like they had been created for each other.

He watched her, face tilted up to the night gazing at the bright stars. Did she feel it too?

He was being foolish. She wasn't available and he wasn't looking for a woman. He liked his life. He only had to think about himself and his animals. Getting his own station was his goal. A woman would just complicate things, and he liked his life uncomplicated. He should just keep his distance from all women. Especially Meghan.

"Darcy, can I ask you something?" Her sweet voice cut at his heart.

"Sure." His voice trembled, scared of just what she wanted to know. He wouldn't be able to lie, even if he wanted too.

"What happened to you? I mean, what was the heartbreak that made you scared of women... and love?" She looked at him with eyebrows raised and an innocent look crossed her face.

He held her gaze contemplating, not wanting to talk about Lisa, ever. But her questioning eyes made it impossible to resist anything she wanted.

He took a deep breath, one thing he knew how to do was control his feelings. He had learnt how a long time ago.

"We went to boarding school in Charters Towers for high school. That's where I met Lisa. We went out for about three years, I thought she was the one. We talked about getting married and working together on a station somewhere." He stared blankly out into the darkness. "Then she came back after holidays, just before our exams and called it quits. She said she had met someone else and they were engaged."

A gasp escaped Meghan's lips, and he turned to look at her.

"I'm so sorry." Her voice was little more than a whisper but it soothed the deep-seated pain that threatened to bubble over.

"The guy was the only son of a grazier out in Winton. They owned a huge station, and he was going to inherit it all. Lisa wasn't going to have to struggle at all with him." He gave her a slight smile.

"Did she end up marrying him?"

"I don't know. We finished our exams, and that was that. I learnt my lesson and never looked back."

She turned to him. "And you haven't dated since?"

"I've avoided anything serious." He gazed at her lovely face. "I don't want a complicated life."

She nodded in understanding. "But, sometimes things have to get a little complicated in order to get what you really want."

CHAPTER 7

*M*eghan opened her eyes in the early light of the morning. Darcy lay sleeping peacefully in the swag next to her. She took the opportunity to study his handsome face.

His bronzed face was speckled with a line of freckles across his nose. His eyelashes were long and dark. His full lips were parted slightly. He smelled of sweat and horse.

His breathing shallowed, and he stirred. She rolled over and turned her head to Lachie's empty swag. She sat up and looked around but couldn't see him amidst the other campers. He had been sound asleep when she and Darcy had returned late last night.

"Morning." Darcy's voice was husky with sleep.

"Morning." She patted down her hair. It probably looked frightful. "I wonder where Lachie is?"

"Probably getting food or puking in the bathroom," Darcy arched his brow. "Want me to look?"

"Would you mind?"

"No worries." He grabbed a change of clothes and his toothbrush and headed to the bathroom.

Meghan changed into black shorts and a purple T-shirt. She brushed her teeth and tied her hair in a bun under her hat. The perfect solution for bed hair.

By the time she'd returned, Lachie and Darcy were in the middle of a heated argument.

"You should have been there." Darcy's voice was low and quiet, but he pointed an accusatory finger at Lachie's chest.

As Meghan approached Lachie walked timidly over to her. "I'm sorry, babe. I haven't seen those guys in ages."

Lachie's behaviour didn't bother her as much as it should. In the past she had been a clingy girlfriend and always needed reassurance that they wouldn't break up with her and abandon her. But Darcy had stayed with her all evening and thinking back, she had barely noticed Lachie's absence.

He lifted her chin up so he could look in her eyes. She saw the apology in his bloodshot eyes.

She shrugged. "Darcy and I had a great night. You missed out on all the fun."

"Yeah, I know." He admitted. "I saw some of the guys this morning. They said you made some new friends."

He leaned in to kiss her, but she pulled back, gagging on his smoky beer breath. "You need to brush your teeth before you try to kiss me again."

He grinned and swatted her ass gently.

From the corner of her eye she saw Darcy walking away.

~

Meghan smiled as they approached the now familiar sign signalling the entrance to Brigadier Station. She was back in familiar surroundings. Home.

Harriet immediately busied herself with laundry and unpacking. Lachie retreated to the office to catch up on work and Darcy was busy unloading Jasper. After unpacking her bag and tidying up Lachie's room, Meghan decided to start on lunch. On her way down the hall, Lachie called to her.

"I just got off the phone with our adjistment property down south. They're pretty concerned our mob may have worms. I need to get down there and sort it out."

She walked around his desk and stood behind him. Her fingers smoothed the tense knots in his neck and shoulders. He needed a shower, he still smelt of sweat and smoke.

"When do you have to go?"

"Pretty much now." Sighing, he leaned back into her hands.

"Do you want me to come?"

"No. You'd be bored and I'll be busy."

She nodded, secretly pleased to not have to leave again just yet. He took her hand and pulled her onto his lap, kissing her briefly. "I'll probably be gone a week or so. I know you only have a few more days before you have to get back to work."

"You won't be able to drive me home then." She was stuck in the outback, without her fiancé. To make matters worse, she was due to start work again in a few days.

"I'm sorry." He hugged her briefly. "Ask Darcy when you see him. He'll be able to get you back to Townsville."

~

Meghan followed a dirt path to a shallow gully surrounded by large gums and coolabah trees. Cockatoos and galahs chirped above her as she followed the gently running stream. Joey trotted up from a path ahead and wagged his tail in hello.

"What are you doing here?" Meghan stopped to pat the dog's head. Darcy's tall figure appeared from the bush and he nodded as he approached her. "Looking for something?"

"Just wandering." Meghan gestured around to the bush. "It's so pretty."

"It's a bugger in a flood. I'm checking the drains for blockages."

"Mind if I join you?"

He shook his head, and they walked side by side in the cool shade of the trees, talking about their childhoods.

"Us boys used to chase each other down here after

lessons." He said. "Dad would find us hours later when it was almost dark. Because we hadn't finished our chores he would be really angry and threaten to spank us if we didn't get back to the house and do them before dinner."

"What was your Dad like?"

Darcy threw her a sharp look. "I'd rather not talk about him."

There was a story there, but she couldn't figure it out. Why didn't they speak about Daniel?

Darcy found a pipe peeking out and went to work making sure they were clear and the water was flowing. Meghan removed her boots and paddled in the shallow, cool water. She watched as a gangly kangaroo hopped lightly between some trees nearby. A small joey followed closely behind. Colourful parrots crooned to each other from their branches of the coolabah trees. She raised her face and closed her eyes, breathing the fresh air deep into her lungs until it filled her soul. The loneliness she had always carried with her was now replaced by an absolute sense of belonging to this beautiful, wild place.

A kookaburra trilled and she looked up to find it.

"Over there." Darcy pointed out the tree where the brown and white bird was perched. Meghan carefully sloshed through the water, closer to Darcy so she could get a better view. She followed where Darcy pointed and saw the bird with the large beak. Darcy closed his hands around his mouth and mimicked its sound. In reply, the kookaburra called back.

"We used to do that all the time as kids," Darcy smiled. "Are you ready to go?"

"Yep, I'll just get my boots." Meghan trudged back to the edge and sat down on a rock. After putting on her socks, she slid her foot into her boot only to feel her toes press against something before a fierce stinging started in her middle toe.

"Ouch." She shrieked, pulling the boot off and grabbing at her foot.

Darcy was by her side in an instant, whipping her sock off and gently holding her swelling foot between his large, calloused hands.

From the corner of her eye, Meghan saw a large spider scuttling away. The deep red stripe on its torso made her shiver.

"Redback." She pointed to Darcy who turned his head to inspect.

"Okay. You'll be alright. I'll call an ambulance and they'll bring anti-venom."

"It hurts so much." Her voice was a ragged whisper. Tears stung her eyes as a wave of pain rolled over her.

Darcy lifted her up in his arms and cradled her gently like a fragile doll. Her head snuggled into his warm neck, his pulse beating against her lips. She focused on that feeling until the pain was only a distant throb.

~

A surge of protectiveness filled Darcy. Holding

Meghan close, he hurried to the ringers' quarters and the closest first aid kit. Her soft whimpers and warm breath against his neck was almost too much to bear. Her floral shampoo surrounded him and she was soft, limp and vulnerable in his arms.

Gently, he placed her on a bed where she instinctively curled into a ball on her side. He made the call to the local paramedics who promised to bring anti-venom out straight-away. The sooner she got the shot, the sooner the pain would cease. In the kitchen, he hunted for pain killers and a bottle of water.

When he returned, she was still in the same foetal position. Her eyes squeezed tight, her hands clenched together against her forehead.

"Sit up, Meghan. Take some pain-killer. I promise it will help."

She turned her dazed face to him, her eyes moist. He helped her up.

After swallowing the pills, she curled up against him. Her head rested against his chest as Darcy placed his arm around her shoulder.

"The pain will be gone soon." He stroked her arm lightly. He would rather endure the pain of ten Redback bites himself than watch her endure this one.

Meghan surfaced from her pain-induced sleep to find herself in Darcy's strong embrace. She savoured the feeling of security it offered and was tempted to close her eyes and sleep some more so she wouldn't have to leave her safe cocoon.

Darcy brushed the loose hair from her face with his large, warm hand and instinctively she moved her cheek into his palm.

"How long have I been out?" She moved off him and stretched. She vaguely remembered the paramedic's visit and the injection they had given her. The pain of the bite had been so intense she had tried to block everything out.

"About two hours. How's the pain?" He asked climbing off the bed and straightening his shirt.

"Mostly gone." Meghan stood and gingerly put weight on her swollen foot. "Still a little tender."

"I'll carry you up to the homestead. Mum's making you soup." He picked her up as though she weighed nothing at all.

Darcy was quiet on the short walk up to the house. Harriet was at the door when they arrived, opening it for him to step through.

"How do you feel, love?" she asked, concern etched on her face.

"Getting better. Sorry for the drama."

Darcy carried her into the living room and laid her on the large couch.

Harriet followed behind closely. "I called Lachie. He said he'd give you a call tonight and see how you're doing."

"Thanks." Meghan accepted the blanket Darcy lay over her.

"I'll get you a glass of water." Harriet hurried out.

"Will you be okay here?" Darcy checked her fore-head for fever with his hand.

Meghan nodded and watched as he turned to leave. "Darcy!"

He turned back to her expectantly.

"Thank you." She smiled up at him. She remem-bered him being next to her the whole time. She had sensed his presence and felt his touch.

He smiled back at her. No words were needed. He had promised to look after her and true to his word, he had.

~

The paramedics had suggested Meghan visit the medical centre the next day for a check-up. As Darcy already had some things to do in town he offered to take her.

Meghan noticed that Darcy's ute was an older model than his brothers, but it was cleaner and better cared for. While Lachie's seats were ripped and the faint stench of cigarette smoke clung to the upholstery, Darcy's had new seat covers and a pine scented air freshener hanging from the rear-view mirror.

Meghan settled herself in for the long drive to town as Darcy turned the volume up on the local radio station. Country music singers sang about heartbreak and loss.

She must have drifted off to sleep, waking as they

pulled into a carpark. The old building which housed the medical clinic was quiet so she was seen quickly by the locum nurse.

"No allergic reaction. Swelling may take a few days to go down. Take painkillers every four hours and watch out for infection," she explained and turned to Darcy. "It's lucky you knew what to do."

"See. I told Harriet we didn't need to come." Meghan hopped down the steps. It hurt when she put too much pressure on her foot.

"Maybe we should get you crutches." Darcy took her weight as he wrapped an arm around her back and helped her into the car.

"No way. I'll be fine."

They drove around the corner to the hardware store. Darcy left the engine running. "Stay here, I won't be long."

He entered the shop, the entrance displayed a wheelbarrow and various tools and advertisements. On the ground was a large, worn, cardboard box, with the word FREE written across the front. As she wondered what was in it a black snout popped out of a hole.

Frowning, she clambered out of the ute and hobbled over to the box. She knelt down and opened the box to find a small black and white puppy peering up at her.

"Well, hello." She picked up the puppy and inspected it for lice and worms. It was newly weaned and seemed clean and healthy. Its colouring and features looked as though it was a border collie cross. Probably meant to be a working dog. She cuddled and played with the pup until Darcy came back out. His hands were full of machinery parts.

"What have you got there?"

"He was in this box."

Darcy put his purchases in the tray of the ute, then walked over and gave the dog a scratch. "Frank. There's a dog in a box out here." He called into the shop.

The bald shop keeper, Frank, came outside and nodded.

"It's the runt from a litter at Kalbarri Station. I said they could leave it here and try their luck getting rid of it."

Alarm trickled through Meghan's veins. "What happens if no one wants him?"

Darcy crouched beside her and patted the puppy. "It's a working dog. Needs a lot of training and room to run around. Lots of work and costly too."

She cuddled it closer. "I can take him to Townsville. Maybe someone will take him there."

"He looks pretty happy with you," said Frank. "Why don't you keep him?"

The thought hadn't occurred to her before, but as soon as he said it, she knew she wanted to keep the little puppy. "Do you think Lachie would mind?"

Darcy shrugged. "I doubt it. We have the space, but I don't know if Lachie knows much about dog training. But, I could help if you need it."

She kissed the dog's wiry hair. "Come on, little fella. You can come live with us."

They walked up the road a little way to the tourist information centre, where Darcy filled up an aluminium bowl Frank had given them with water. Meghan watched the puppy dart around the water fountain and idly read the inscription around it.

"Now the stock have started dying, for the lord has sent a drought;

But we're sick of prayers and Providence – we're going to do without;

With the derricks up above us and the solid earth below,

We are waiting at the lever for the word to let her go.

Sinking down, deeper down,

Oh, we'll sink it deeper down."

"Song of the Artesian Water. By Banjo Patterson."

Suddenly the puppy bounded back to her and obediently, sat at her feet as though she had called him.

"Hey, fella. You like that poem?" He closed his eyes blissfully as she stroked his back. "Do you like Banjo Patterson?" As if in response, the dog started thumping his tail.

"Banjo. Is that your name?"

Darcy put the bowl of water next to her and the dog thirstily slurped it up.

"He's chosen his own name." Meghan smiled proudly. "Darcy, meet Banjo."

Darcy crouched down. "Gidday, Banjo."

Banjo licked his face. A wet, slobbery kiss.

Meghan started laughing as Darcy gently pushed the puppy away and wiped his face with the bottom of his shirt, revealing his flat, smooth stomach.

"Yep, definitely needs some training," he chuckled.

~

Meghan tightened her seatbelt, her heart thumping double time as the single engine Cessna purred to life under Darcy's control. "You sure you can fly this to Townsville?" she spoke into the headset's mouth piece.

"Trust me." Darcy's voice came through her headset low and loud.

She looked over to see him watching her. His eyes crinkled mischievously like he knew something she didn't.

"Have you been in a plane like this before?"

"Not one this small." She glanced back at the four seats behind her. Banjo was inside a dog cage on the floor. He was dozing happily, seemingly unaware of his owner's nerves.

Meghan had already fallen in love with Banjo and being away from him at such a young age, was not an option for her. In Townsville she would get his health checked and have him microchipped. She could also start some basic training before they returned to the station for good.

Meghan took aerial shots of Brigadier Station as

they flew low over it, circling around so she could get all vantages.

Darcy pointed out sites and she watched the forbidding flat landscape pass beneath them. He had hidden talents up every sleeve. Just when she thought she had him worked out, he surprised her again.

She had to raise her voice to be heard over the thrum of the engines. "When did you learn to fly?"

"I got licensed through the aero club in Julia Creek. I actually wanted to be a pilot in the air force when I was younger." Darcy replied.

"So, what stopped you?" Meghan asked.

"Dad wouldn't allow it. He said I had to stay on the land and help Lachie." A muscle in his jaw twitched. "No one would dare disobey Daniel McGuire."

"Really? What do you mean?" she puzzled.

He shook his head. "Never mind." Daniel's name was rarely mentioned, and she wondered if there was a family secret. The fact Darcy didn't want to talk about it confirmed her suspicions.

"What did you want to do when you were younger?" he asked.

"I wanted to be a painter." She smiled wistfully. "I took every art class possible at school. But I also love animals so it was a tough decision."

"Do you still paint?"

"Not for a long time." The familiar urge to pick up a paintbrush had her fingers twitching. It had been years since she had painted anything.

"You want a go?" His voice pulled her back.

"At what? Flying?" She turned to him with wide eyes.

He nodded. "Yeah. Take the controls."

"Okay." She put her hands on the wheel in front of her and under Darcy's direction she turned them slightly. The plane turned with it. She straightened up again, and he put his arms behind his head and leant back.

"You're flying."

"I am. This is so cool."

After a few minutes, Meghan's mobile rang. Darcy took back the controls while Meghan checked the message. Mobile service was unreliable this far west.

"My friend, Jodie is picking me up from the airport," she told Darcy while finishing her message. "That reminds me, what's your mobile number?"

"I don't have a mobile," he said.

"Seriously? No mobile?" Meghan pondered the possibility. "What about an email?"

He shook his head apologetically. "No need for one."

"Lachie has a mobile."

"Lachie has to have a mobile for station business. Besides, he has you to call."

Before long they were entering Townsville airspace. Darcy communicated with the airport tower and was given permission to land. He guided the plane in smoothly and taxied to the designated bay.

"Come meet my friend," Meghan said, as they descended the stairs of the aircraft.

"Okay, I've got some time."

They headed toward the tall blonde dressed in a short skirt and revealing top. Jodie liked to make the most of her assets.

"That's what I thought you'd look like," Darcy commented as Meghan pointed her out.

"She's Lachie's type?" Meghan asked as she laughed at Darcy's comment. Lachie had met Jodie a few times, and although they were friendly to each other, Lachie had never seemed to take particular notice of her looks.

Jodie gave Darcy a good look over. "Hello."

"Hi." Meghan watched as he squirmed slightly under her friend's rakish gaze. Jodie appreciated a well-formed male body and Darcy certainly fit into that category. In his blue-checked shirt, jeans and boots, he looked like a real man who was good with his hands and not afraid to get dirty. Lachie gave out a similar vibe, but he knew it and made it work for him. Darcy was completely unaware of his appeal.

"So, um, you're the Matron of Honour?"

Jodie dramatically put her hand to her chest and feigned horror. "Maid not matron. Heaven's, I'm not old enough to be a matron of anything."

Meghan placed her hand on Darcy's arm. "Don't worry about her. She's a bit dramatic."

He relaxed under her gaze. "Of course, I'm sorry. Guess that's almost as bad as asking your age."

Jodie laughed her high pitched, flirty laugh. "Oh, I like you. We're going to get on so well."

Darcy raised his eyebrows before checking his watch. "I better head off if I want to get in before dark."

"See you at the wedding." Jodie smiled suggestively.

"Thanks again." Meghan stepped forward and hugged him briefly.

"No problem. Bye, Meghan."

Both girls watched him walk away, hypnotized by the sway of his hips.

"What's with the hugging?" Jodie playfully nudged her friend. "You hate hugging."

"I don't hate it. It's okay with people I know." Meghan waved as the Cessna taxied out of sight. "Darcy and I get on really well, and we have heaps in common."

"Yes, but is he single?"

"Yes, but he doesn't like the city much."

"Who cares I only need an hour or so. He's hot. Possibly even better looking than Lachie."

"You think so?" Meghan mentally compared the two.

"Toss up."

"So how did you like the outback?" Jodie asked as they walked towards her car.

"I loved it. It's so far away from everything. They only go into Julia Creek once a month or so and stock up on groceries. They get milk and perishables delivered when they run out. Harriet has to cook a lot."

"Forget Indian takeout there then. Think you can hack it? Really?"

"I would want to move there even if I wasn't

marrying Lachie. It feels like home to me." Certainty filled Meghan and she smiled.

~

Darcy landed back at the airstrip just as the sun was setting. He closed the hangar doors behind him and watched as the last flickers of orange disappeared below the horizon. Meghan would have loved that sunset. He suddenly felt very alone; like he had lost his best friend. Actually, Meghan probably was the best friend he had ever had. In such a short time, he had shared things with her that he had never thought to tell anyone before.

He stopped by the horses to check and feed them before heading back to the house. Joey was there waiting, and he looked at him quizzically as if asking where the mistress was.

"You miss them too, don't you?" He patted the dog, and Joey licked his hand affectionately.

Harriet was setting the table for two when Darcy entered the kitchen.

"Safe trip?" she asked.

"Yep. I met Meghan's maid of honour."

"Oh?" Harriet raised her eyebrows

"She's…" Darcy racked his brain for the appropriate adjective. "A real city girl."

"Oh." Harriet nodded in understanding. They had seen plenty of women come out from the city with dreams of marrying a wealthy grazier and living a life of leisure in the country but still being able to fly back to the city whenever they ran out of eye cream or wanted to visit the theatre. Few of them ever stayed around longer than a few months.

Darcy had nothing against city girls, though. They were the result of their upbringing just as country girls were the result of theirs. Men were the same. Each to their own, was his motto.

He washed his hands in the kitchen sink. "I'm going to fix up the ringers' quarters and move there before the wedding." He had been thinking about it since Lachie had announced the engagement. "The newly-weds won't want me cramping their privacy."

"Yes, I thought I might start looking for a place in town." Harriet agreed then looked around at her home. "I'll talk to Meghan about it next time she comes."

Darcy carried his plate of fried chicken to the table and sat next to his mother. He glanced at the empty seat Meghan had occupied. "You think they will make a good couple?"

"I think she will be a wonderful daughter-in-law."

Darcy nodded in agreement but said nothing further on the subject.

CHAPTER 8

Soft music played in the bridal shop, lulling customers into dreams of fairy-tale weddings and happily-ever-afters. Meghan was not immune to its effect, especially when the room smelled like newly-opened roses on a spring day. She had no idea what style wedding dress she would suit, just that it had to be simple and elegant. "Absolutely no frills or taffeta," she reminded Jodie who seemed intent on choosing the most revealing, girly dresses she could find. "Look for a dress for me, not you."

Jodie slowly moved to stand beside her friend. "Umm, Meghan?"

"Yeah?"

"You don't think this is all happening a bit quickly do you?" Her voice was quiet.

Meghan frowned wondering what had brought this conversation on. "Where's this coming from?"

"You've saved me from my share of bad relationships over the years, so let's just say it's my turn to look after you." Jodie fingered some white lace of a dress near her. "I mean, I know you've always dreamed about being married and having a family of your own, but are you sure Lachie is the one?"

Meghan reached out and pulled her childhood friend into a tight hug. "Thank you for looking out for me. But I know what I'm doing."

"I know you wish your Mum was here. I do too. She was like another mother to me. I know she would want me to make sure you're doing the right thing." When the two women finally came apart they were both wiping tears away. Jodie had been Meghan's rock when her mother had died. She had helped with the funeral arrangements and had stayed with her friend for weeks, making sure she ate and dressed each day.

"Mum is here. In spirit." Meghan smiled. "Now, help me find a dress."

They turned back to the racks. "What are the boys going to wear? Jeans and a T-shirt?"

"No." She ran her hand over a lacy dress on the rack she was working her way through. "I'm going to buy them both a nice suit and white shirt. No ties though, it's too formal."

"Do you have their sizes? We could do that next."

Meghan face lit up suddenly, and she pulled out an ivory satin dress. She walked over to a mirror and held it against herself.

Jodie's eyes lit up as she clapped her hand over her mouth. "Try it on."

Meghan took off her T-shirt and shorts then carefully dropped the dress over her head. It whispered as it slipped down her body, as though it had been made for her. The amazed look on Jodie's face said it all.

Turning to the mirror, Meghan took her first look. The dress had a loose cowl neckline and diamantes on the shoulder straps. It clung to her body like a second skin accentuating her curves. She piled her hair on top of her head exposing the diamantes more brilliantly.

"It's perfect." Jodie placed her arm around Meghan's shoulder in a show of solidarity.

"It is," Meghan murmured. Her eyes stung as she gazed at herself in her wedding dress. She wished Mum was here. This was a moment in a girl's life when she needed her mother. At least she had Jodie—her substitute sister.

The shop assistant had been quietly watching from the shadows. She came forward now and studied the size. "It's a perfect fit."

Meghan smiled before she remembered their earlier conversation. "The boy's sizes! Pass me my phone, and I'll call Harriet. She'll know."

"Good idea." Jodie shuffled through her friend's bag before finding the mobile. She handed her the phone.

"I'll give you two a few minutes." The assistant smiled before leaving the room.

Meghan found the number and waited as it rang.

"Brigadier Station." The dulcet tones of Darcy's familiar voice caused her breath to quicken.

"Darcy, I wasn't expecting you to answer. Where's Harriet?"

There was a short pause before he answered. "She's in town on wedding business."

"Oh, I thought something might be wrong. What are you doing home so early in the day?"

"Early lunch. The tractor broke down, and I'm about to fix it."

"Right. Of course." Another hidden talent; Darcy seemed able to fix and do everything.

"How are you?" he asked.

It had been almost a week since Darcy had flown her to Townsville. He had been on her mind a lot, and she was secretly pleased to have the chance to speak to him now.

"I'm good, thanks. Actually, Jodie and I are wedding dress shopping." She giggled. "I'm wearing the perfect dress right now."

"Is it all frilly?" She could hear his warm smile in his voice.

"No. It's satin actually." She winked at Jodie who was sitting on the couch watching her.

Another long pause. "I'm sure it's beautiful. Lachie will love it." He suddenly sounded very formal, and she wondered if she had said something wrong.

"So, I'm going to buy you a suit for the wedding. What size are you?"

"I have a suit."

"You do?" Meghan asked surprised.

"I don't wear it much, but it's there."

"It's not some weird old suit that belonged to your grandfather, is it?"

Darcy chuckled. "No, it's a plain black suit with a white shirt. I even own a blue tie."

"Nice. The tie would bring out the colour of your eyes." Meghan had a vision of him at the altar. Waiting. For her?

She shook her head. "Does it fit?"

"Yes, it fits. I promise."

"Okay. I believe you. You said you never lie." Warmth settled in her stomach.

"That's right. When are you coming back? Shadow's almost ready to have her foal."

"Is she? Maybe I could drive up this weekend." Meghan only had a few more shifts left at work before she finished up. She could drive up Saturday morning, stay the night and drive back Sunday.

"I could pick you up Friday. Lachie should be home by then."

Lachie, was still away with the agistment heard. They had only spoken a couple of times briefly as the reception was always crackly. He had, however, organized a beautiful bouquet of flowers be delivered to her house the day after she returned home. Her heart had fluttered at the gesture. He could be so sweet and romantic when he made an effort.

"I don't want to inconvenience you."

"No inconvenience at all." His voice now sounding intimately close.

"Can I fly the plane again?"

"You want lessons now?" he teased, "Sure, you can fly for a bit."

"Excellent. Call my mobile before you leave so I can get to the airport and meet you."

"No worries. See you then, Meghan."

"Bye, Darcy." She ended the call. Jodie was watching her.

"Nice to know a guy with a plane! Shame Lachie won't be there, or you could join the mile-high club!"

"Jodie!" Meghan threw the phone next to her on the couch and turned back to the mirror. She studied herself and thought of Darcy and his blue tie. Visions of him standing next to her, holding her hand crossed her mind. Then suddenly another imagined figure was standing next to her holding her other hand.

This one was Lachie.

Her fiancé. The one she was supposed to marry.

~

About to take off. ETA 2 hrs. Darcy

A text message from Darcy. Meghan tried to swallow down the butterflies in her throat. He had gotten a mobile since their last meeting.

Welcome to the 21st Century. C U soon.

She left her car in the carpark at Townsville Airport and waited for the Cessna to appear in the sky. She spotted its red stripe and watched as Darcy landed and taxied over to an empty bay. Sitting in the cockpit, he looked very professional in his aviator sunglasses and headset. He smiled when he saw her, and she waved back. Banjo pulled excitedly on his leash. His tail swishing violently.

"Hello!" She hugged Darcy when he'd descended the stairs. "How was the flight?"

"Smooth. Been here long?" He pushed his sunglasses up into his hair. The deep blue of his eyes startled her again. She'd forgotten how intense their colour was.

"Yeah, but we like watching the planes so we came early." She gestured to Banjo who was jumping up, eager for attention. Darcy didn't disappoint. Crouching down he received a sloppy kiss from the pup.

"Still got some training to do." He raised an eyebrow at Meghan, who stifled a laugh.

"Just a bit."

Darcy nodded at her luggage. A large suitcase and three cardboard boxes. "How long are you staying?'

"Didn't you hear? I'm moving in." Meghan joked. "I thought I might as well leave some stuff there. Is that okay?"

"It's all good. Hop up." Darcy stood aside and loaded the luggage as she and Banjo climbed aboard.

True to his word, Darcy took the time to point out what the buttons and switches did and how the plane worked. He even had her do some of the checks and start the engine.

She was staggered at how complicated it all was and her respect for Darcy and his many talents increased.

Once in the air, she watched Townsville disappear below her.

"How's your Mum?" Meghan asked when he gave the okay for conversation.

"She's good. Helping me out while Lachie's gone. We've also got one of Lachie's friends to help us out for the next few weeks while we vaccinate the herd."

"Will he stay on the station somewhere?"

"In the ringers' quarters. There are four bedrooms, a bathroom, and a kitchen so he can have one," Darcy explained glancing over at her. "I'm fixing one up for myself."

"But you live in the main house." Meghan frowned.

"You won't want me living there when you and Lachie get married. Besides, you'll need the room when you have kids." She thought she could hear a hint of something in his voice.

"Kids are a long way off." Meghan paused as she realised this was a topic she and Lachie still hadn't discussed. They would need an heir to the station at some point. After meeting Jamie, she knew she wanted children one day.

"You want kids?" she asked Darcy.

"Sure. But nieces and nephews will do me for a while." He smiled back.

Meghan thought about all the things she and Lachie had forgotten to talk about. What would happen to Harriet? Where would the kids go to school? Would he still travel all the time?

"So, you got a phone." Meghan changed the subject.

"A satellite phone, like Lachie's. Made sense to have two."

"Next thing you'll be setting up a Facebook account. Or online dating." She laughed shakily. An image of him trolling online dating sites for a woman, made her stomach churn.

"I don't think so." He shook his head slowly. No, Darcy would never do that. That wasn't his way. "I'll be the fun bachelor uncle to your kids. I'm happy on my own."

Her heart sank for him. She knew what it was like to be alone and she wouldn't wish that on anyone. At least he would have his mother, Lachie and herself for company.

"Surely if the right girl came along..." She started but stopped when her stomach churned again.

Darcy sent her a bemused glance.

"Jodie made a comment about Lachie being here so we could join the mile-high club." Meghan blurted out, then bit her tongue. "Sorry, too much info."

"Ah yeah. Thanks, but I don't need to imagine my brother doing that in my plane." They both laughed and chatted about the station's irrigation system and the next campdrafting event Darcy was entering.

The sun was setting as they approached the airstrip on Brigadier Station. Meghan looked out the window and spotted Lachie's ute. She frowned; she hadn't expected to see him until they had driven back to the homestead.

Darcy landed the plane and taxied it into the hangar.

Joey yapped as he saw his owner and Meghan descend the stairs. Lachie waited patiently next to the dog, a welcoming smile on his face.

Banjo excitedly ran off to play with Joey and Meghan stepped into Lachie's waiting embrace. "What are you doing here?"

"I missed you," he whispered into her hair.

Meghan pulled back, aware Darcy was standing next to her.

"All good?" Lachie nodded to the airplane, but Meghan sensed he was referring to more than just the flight.

"Yep. Everything's fine here. I'll take Banjo home." Darcy nodded. "See you at the house."

"Cheers." Lachie picked up Meghan's bag and led her to his waiting ute.

Meghan turned to watch Darcy bend down and pat the dogs.

Lachie drove them a short distance in the dark. She couldn't tell where they were, it was all unfamiliar with only a sliver of moonlight. He pulled up abruptly next to large gum tree.

"Why have we stopped?"

"You'll see." He smiled and climbed out of the car.

Meghan followed him and watched as he spread a picnic blanket under the tree and placed a battery-operated lantern in a corner.

"Sit down." Lachie motioned and turned off the

headlights. When he returned, he sat next to her and held out his enclosed hands. "Pick one."

"This one." She tapped his right hand. He opened it, but there was nothing there.

"Pick the other one." He laughed.

She touched that hand, and when he opened, she gasped at the sight of a silver ring. She picked it up and studied it next to the light. The round diamond was simple and classic.

"It's lovely."

"Here." Lachie took the ring and slid it on her left hand. It was a size too big, but he didn't appear to notice.

Meghan took his face in her hands and kissed him sweetly. "Thank you."

"You're welcome." He smiled back.

Absently, she rubbed the ring with her finger. Lachie shuffled closer and Meghan rested more comfortably against his solid chest. He had used after-shave. It was the same fragrance he wore in the city. It reminded her of the happy times they had spent there, just the two of them. He was different then. Or maybe she was different then. Something was different.

He swept her hair away from her neck and kissed her nape. Usually, his touch and kisses sent her into a frenzy of desire, but this time, it seemed forced.

"We should go. Harriet will be expecting us," she whispered into the night, expecting him to argue and continue kissing her.

Lachie surprised her with his quick agreement.

"Yeah, I'm tired. It's been a long week." He yawned as if to prove his point.

Without another word, they gathered up the rug and lantern and drove home.

~

Darcy expected to see Meghan's face flushed and her hair messed when she returned. He pushed the thought from his mind. He had to keep reminding himself they were engaged and could do what they wanted. He opened the door and was surprised to hear their voices. They were back already.

Harriet saw him approach "Look Darcy. Lachie just gave it to her." Harriet pointed to Meghan's long, slender hand.

Darcy glanced over and frowned. "Nice." A ring. It's official now.

He caught his mother's eye with a questioning look. She just smiled and shook her head knowingly. Darcy strode to the fridge and pulled out a beer. He took a long drink before returning to his family.

"I think the calves might come early this year," he said to Lachie as he took his seat at the dinner table.

"The agistment cows too," he replied. "It's going to be a busy time."

Harriet and Meghan sat in their assigned seats, Meghan next to Lachie and Harriet.

"Dig in, you must be hungry." Harriet gestured to the food.

There was roast chicken, boiled potatoes, carrots, and beans. Meghan waited while the men continued their conversation and piled their plates high with food.

Harriet and Meghan exchanged a knowing look and smile.

"Harriet, I don't want you to feel as though you are not welcome to stay here after the wedding," Meghan said quietly to her friend. "I'll still need your help and your company."

Harriet grinned back. "Thank you, honey. I'll stay for as long as you want me. But I don't want to step on toes, so you kick me out at any time!"

"Just make sure she's taught you how to make her pavlova first," Lachie said with his mouth full.

"And her fruit cake," Darcy joined in. The boys both moaned pleasurably at the memory and rubbed their stomachs.

Meghan laughed, "And how to care for the roses, of course."

Harriet patted her hand affectionately. "Welcome home, Meghan."

CHAPTER 9

*I*t was a quarter to three in the morning when Darcy opened the door to Lachie's room. He wasn't comfortable doing this, but Meghan had made him promise to get her, even if it meant waking her up. He tiptoed into the room and spied Meghan lying on her side; Lachie was sprawled on his stomach, his head turned away.

Darcy bent down, his face close to Meghan's. He could hear her breathing deeply and he wondered briefly what she was dreaming about. He placed his hand on her bare shoulder. Her singlet strap had fallen loose during the night.

She was warm under his touch, despite the chilly night. He shook her gently and whispered her name.

Her eyes fluttered open, and she smiled dreamily at him. "Darcy?"

"Shadow's in labor. She's about to have the foal."

Meghan sat up quickly. "I'll be ready in a sec."

Darcy waited outside her door with a torch.

She joined him quickly in jeans and a sweater. She put on her boots and followed him to the stable.

They leaned over the stable door, careful not to interrupt. Shadow was circling the stall, blowing heavily. Her head was downcast with concentration, her tail whipping from side to side.

"Is she in pain? Is something wrong?" Meghan asked, although her instincts told her this was normal.

"No. She's doing well. It won't be long now."

They watched the mare take a few more turns before collapsing onto the soft hay Darcy had spread out. She lay on her side, and Meghan watched in amazement as the contractions rippled over her belly.

Meghan held her breath as amniotic fluid gushed out and two hooves, still inside the sack became visible. Meghan had seen plenty of animals give birth before. She had even studied foaling at TAFE, but she had never seen it live before.

Tension filled the air. Shadow was pushing hard, but nothing seemed to be happening. Darcy must have sensed it too, as he pushed the door open and stepped cautiously inside.

He felt the mare's bulging stomach. "She needs some help."

"What can I do?" Meghan asked, wishing she had more equine training.

"Put on some gloves." Darcy pointed to a box behind her. She rolled the long plastic gloves over her hands and up past her elbows.

Darcy stayed at Shadow's belly, his hands gently massaging. "Can you pull on the hooves. Wait until she starts pushing, though."

Meghan nodded and knelt at the horse's tail. As the contractions came, she pulled gently on the foal. Inch by inch it slipped further out. After several minutes the rest of the foal and amniotic fluid was released in a great gush.

Darcy inspected the sack before breaking it open and releasing the still foal.

"Let's get out of the way." He led her back out of the stall, where she removed her gloves and washed her hands. By the time she returned, Shadow was licking her new brown foal.

"It's so cute." They watched the foal try to stand on shaky, thin legs.

Darcy stood next to Meghan, his hands on his waist. He still wore yesterday's clothes and looked tired from the long night. Even as dishevelled as he was he looked handsome and proud as he gazed at the new edition.

"Good job," she said and patted him on the back.

He gazed down at her, his eyes bright.

"Thank you for the help. Your vet nursing skills are coming in handy."

She smiled, her shoulders back. She was thrilled to have been part of the event. "You obviously knew what you were doing."

"I grew up around animals. Not much I haven't seen." He grinned. The tension had left his body now, and he looked relaxed but tired.

"I need a cuppa," he said as they headed back to the house. It was nearing sunrise, and there was no point going to sleep now with work to do.

"I'll make it. You rest for a bit," Meghan said as they removed their boots at the front door.

The house was quiet, Harriet and Lachie still asleep. Meghan made two cups of tea, remembering Darcy liked his black and sweet. She carried the cups to the veranda where he was slumped in a chair, feet stretched out his head back. His eyes were closed.

Meghan put the cups on the table next to his chair and sat watching him doze peacefully. As the sun rose she watched the sky illuminate. Orange beams spilled over the parched, dry earth. As another sunny day began in the North Queensland outback.

Meghan was overcome by the night's excitement. It was wonderful to be alive and to be here on the station. She wanted life to stay just as it was, right this moment. It was absolutely perfect.

~

Meghan had never ridden a motor bike, so Lachie decided it was time that changed. After breakfast, he took her for a spin around the paddock.

She could see the appeal of the bike, after all they cost less than horses and the terrain was flat and bikes managed it perfectly. But the engine heat and exhaust fumes just didn't inspire her the way horseback riding did.

They rounded the corner and Lachie brought the quad bike to a stop in front of the house. He waited for Meghan to dismount behind him, then swung his leg over and looked up at her.

"Fun, huh?" he beamed.

"Um, yeah," Meghan forced a smile. The ride on the quad bike had been mostly scary as Lachie sped along the fields and took corners too quickly in an attempt to show off. She could see why Darcy preferred his horse to these dangerous quad bikes.

It was becoming obvious how few things they shared in common and how little they actually knew about each other. She couldn't help but compare him to Darcy, who she had only met a few weeks ago, but already knew more about than her own fiancé. Meghan quickly brushed the thoughts from her mind and reminded herself that she loved Lachie and that was enough. Harriet was laying lunch out on the table when they came in. Freshly baked bacon and egg pie and salad.

The three of them started their meals and were soon joined by Darcy.

"How's the foal?" Meghan asked him. She was eager to visit the newborn.

"Good. He's got a white patch on his head, shaped like a diamond." Darcy washed his hands in the kitchen sink.

"Is it a filly or colt?" Harriet asked.

"A colt." Darcy sat across from Meghan and served himself. "You get the honours of naming him."

"Me? Why?"

"Why not? Just pick something good. He'll be a campdrafting horse."

Meghan thought of the newborn foal she had met during the night, but no good names came to mind. "I'll think about it."

Darcy nodded and started to eat.

"Oh, Dylan called from next door. He wanted to know if you were keen for a camp out at the creek tonight?" Harriet said to the men.

"Yeah, sounds good," Lachie said.

"Sounds like fun." Meghan smiled.

"I might ride Jasper and meet you guys there," Darcy said.

"Can I ride Molly then?" Meghan turned to Darcy for permission. He nodded nonchalantly.

"Yeah, and I'll come out later with the ute." Lachie agreed. "Might as well sleep out there."

"Don't forget the swags then."

"And beer. I definitely can't forget the beer!" Lachie grinned.

"So, we'll sleep out there?" Meghan clarified.

"Yep. It's a full moon. It'll be nice." Lachie said as he rose from the table. He kissed the top of Meghan's head. "See you out there."

"I'll call Maddie and let her know," Harriet said and went to make the call.

Alone again, Darcy turned to Meghan. "You alright with that?"

"Of course, just a little worried about snakes," she admitted.

"We'll check the swag before you get in," Darcy smiled. "It's okay, I won't let anything hurt you."

Meghan's shoulder relaxed. She could trust Darcy to keep her safe.

"We'll ride out about four. Bring a swimsuit, the river's still full enough to swim in."

Molly cantered along the sweeping plains kicking up dust below her hooves. Under Darcy's instructions, Jasper kept a good pace with the older mare so they rode side by side.

Meghan loved the colours of this country. The rich brown soil under the endless deep blue sky. She yearned to mix her paints and replicate the colours on canvas. Out here, under the slamming North Queensland sun, was exactly where she wanted to be. This was her home. She belonged out here in the bush.

Turning, she watched Darcy ride. He was more himself in the saddle than at any other time. He and Jasper had a deeper relationship than Darcy had with anyone else as though they could read each other's mind. It was as obvious now as in the campdrafting ring.

With the sun in their eyes, they approached a

cluster of eucalypt trees. Their tangy, sharp scent hung in the air. Meghan breathed it in deeply. The smell reminded her of her brief childhood days on the stud farm where she remembered climbing huge eucalypts and watching the horses roam grassy paddocks.

A wide, deep creek emerged surrounded by rocks and grey stones. The water was green-tinged but sparkled enticingly in the sunlight.

Darcy pulled his horse up at the water's edge and dismounted letting Jasper drink from the creek. Meghan followed his lead.

Parrots called to each other from the tops of the coolabah trees. The bright-coloured birds zigzagged between the branches, shaking leaves to the ground. Meghan watched their performance for a few moments before becoming aware of Darcy watching her.

"The others should be here soon." His voice was husky. "We should get some firewood."

Darcy was careful not to let Meghan wander from his sight as they collected sticks and dead branches. The decaying foliage was just the sort of habitat snakes would curl up and hide in. She didn't complain about the job when she came back flushed from the work, her clothes covered in leaves and debris. He had to admit that every day Meghan looked more and more like she belonged out here. He pushed these thoughts aside before they went any further. He knew he shouldn't be thinking about her at all.

He looked up at the sound of an approaching vehicle. Dylan's ute was coming up the track. He dumped his pile of firewood at the flat site where they would camp and walked over to greet his friends. Meghan followed him.

Dylan shook his hand and greeted him with a broad smile before turning to Meghan "It's nice to meet you. Congratulations on the engagement."

"Thank you," Meghan replied, her face was flushed from exercise. Maddie stood next to her.

"You made short work of that." Dylan slapped Darcy on the back. "I didn't even know you were seeing anyone."

He ignored the trip in his pulse. "That's because I'm not. Meghan is Lachie's fiancé."

An awkward pause occurred as Dylan looked between Meghan and Darcy.

"Too much going on in there to remember who's marrying who," Maddie exclaimed as she ruffled Dylan's short dark hair.

"Sorry. Where is the groom then?" He looked around.

"He's coming later in the ute," Darcy explained as the two women opened the car's back door where Maddie's son was sitting.

Darcy tried to concentrate on his conversation with his old friend, but he was more interested in Meghan's interactions with the baby.

"Hi, Jamie!" Meghan cooed as Maddie lifted the little boy from his seat. He looked at Meghan and gurgled at her.

"Emma's at home with Mum. She's too girly for a campout!" Maddie sighed. "Would you mind holding him while I get his food?" Meghan nodded enthusiastically and took the small boy.

She held Jamie against her chest. He grabbed onto loose tendrils of her hair which had come loose from her ponytail. Watching her with the baby stirred something deep within him, and he realised how much he wanted a family himself. He had decided after Lisa that he would never have a family or a wife. But now he was starting to reconsider the idea.

"Let's get the fire going," Dylan suggested. Darcy nodded in agreement, needing a distraction. Soon things were set up and ready.

"Anyone else keen for a swim?" Maddie asked the group. It was a warm afternoon, so everyone agreed.

Darcy followed his friends into the cool water after changing into his striped swim shorts.

His breath caught as he saw Meghan approach the water in a blue floral bikini. Her ivory skin was bare and exposed. He tried to look away, but couldn't.

Gingerly she stepped into the cool water, and when it was up to her waist, she dived in and swam beneath the surface. Popping her head up slowly in front of Maddie and Jamie, he giggled when she playfully squirted water at him.

Darcy's heart melted. Damn, he was falling for his brother's girl.

~

Meghan and Maddie sat on the sand and played with Jaime while the men stoked the fire. The women chatted easily and Meghan felt reassured she had another friend in the outback.

"It's so nice to have another woman to talk to." Maddie smiled broadly. "It gets so tedious with just Dylan and the kids. Our Guuvie, Briar is great, but she's still young and single. I can't complain about men to her."

Meghan laughed. "We can share stories and compare their bad habits."

"Yes! Exactly." Maddie clasped her hands together. "It's going to be great having you as a neighbour. Just a couple of weeks to go before the wedding."

"Yeah, it's coming up quick." Meghan took a deep, steadying breath. Every time she thought about the wedding she would tremble with nerves.

"It's so exciting. The first wedding at Brigadier Station."

Lachie arrived with the beer and swags as promised. After briefly catching up with Dylan, he brought two beers over to the women and sat down next to Meghan.

"Isn't Jamie gorgeous?" she remarked, hoping he would fall in love with him as much as she had.

"Yeah, but he's got a while to go before he's as handsome as me." Lachie teased.

Meghan smiled but noticed he didn't pay much attention to the baby. Perhaps he didn't like children after all. Of course, he would love his own.

The smell of burning wood cleared the scent of dust from her nose. The group sat around the campfire cooking sausages threaded on sticks over the open flames. When they were cooked through they covered them with tomato sauce and wrapped them in bread. It tasted like the country to Meghan. They washed dinner down with cold beers from the cooler as they were entertained by screeching cockatoos flying between trees, as the sun went down and the evening cooled off.

"We should get going." Maddie hugged her tired, fussing son. "See you at the wedding if not before."

They said their goodbyes and waved as their friends left. Feeling sadly empty Meghan went to the horses and hugged Molly's warm neck finding comfort in her soft whickering.

She would return to Townsville tomorrow and the next time she came out would be for the wedding in two weeks' time. Harriet had organized most things. Chairs and tables were being brought in. Alcohol and drinks were in fridges and Harriet would be spending the days leading up baking and cooking. They had booked a celebrant for a morning service and lunch to follow. Allowing travellers plenty of time to get there and get home before dark. Meghan planned to drive up the day before with Jodie who would be her only guest.

Lachie had suggested delaying a honeymoon and that didn't bother Meghan. She wanted to get settled into Brigadier and into her new lifestyle.

The night grew late, and they were soon yawning. Lachie, buzzed from quite a few beers, retreated to his swag first.

Meghan gnawed on her nails as she eyed up the swag. "Check it for me?" she asked Darcy.

He opened it and shone a torch inside. "All good."

Meghan climbed in and warmed up almost immediately. She lay on her back, the cool breeze floating over her face as she stared up at the sky.

Darcy doused the fire and lay out his swag next to hers.

In the darkness, the moon hung bright and huge. The sky was dotted everywhere with stars.

"Can you see the Southern Cross?" Darcy asked.

"Up there." Meghan pointed to the five stars which made a diamond shape. "That bright one there is Venus."

"Where?" Darcy moved closer to Meghan so their heads were touching. "That bright one?"

"Yes. Oh, look!" A shooting star streaked through the sky.

"Make a wish," Darcy whispered.

Meghan closed her eyes and smiled as she thought a wish. When she opened them again, she caught Darcy watching her.

He looked away quickly. "Get some sleep."

She looked back at the moon in wonderment.

"Darcy."

"Yeah?" he turned toward her.

"I know what we should name the colt," she whispered. "Moonshine."

She could hear him exhale. "That's a great name."

Exhaustion pressed against Darcy's shoulders but sleep evaded him. He couldn't ignore the growing doubts in his head that said there was more to life than early mornings, lonely nights and a damnable never-ending drought.

Meghan was the perfect woman. She was intelligent, compassionate, gentle and loving. His heart squeezed thinking about her playing with Jaime and even Banjo. She was the type of woman he would enjoy spending his life with. He shook his head. He couldn't have Meghan, she was taken. Maybe he could find another woman, just like her. Who was he fooling? He would never find another woman like Meghan. She was something else.

Damn. Lachie was one lucky man. He should appreciate her more.

Darcy had spent most of his childhood jealous of his brother. He always got the new things first. The new clothes, boots, bikes, utes. Noah and Darcy had always had to wait for the hand-me-downs. Not to mention their father's love and affection. Lachie was the heir so he got the best of their father. Daniel always saved his nice, patient side for Lachie. He'd always exhausted it by the time he got home and the younger brothers bore the brunt of his frustration and rage. Daniel McGuire had been a very different father to Lachie than his younger sons.

Daniel was gone now, and with him the tension that had always hung over the house had disappeared too. Lachie had stepped up to his new role and seemed to be coping with the responsibilities. Add to that an amazing wife and Lachie was about to have it all.

Darcy rolled onto his side, away from Meghan. He didn't need any more reminders about what he didn't have in life.

CHAPTER 10

*B*etween the curlew's eerie shrieks and the rustling sounds of small critters in the bush, Meghan didn't sleep well. When the sun finally threw light on the camp site, Meghan sat up and watched it, soaking in the beauty of the light streaking through the trees. Lachie was snoring loudly, and Darcy had turned away from her. Climbing out of the swag, Meghan wandered to the creek and splashed water on her face. She breathed the fresh morning air, letting it deep into her lungs. Hearing a strange noise, she hurried back to find Lachie crouched over a bush. The smell of vomit made her stomach turn.

"You okay?" Meghan knelt beside him and rubbed his back. Obviously, Lachie had had a few too many. He was pale and sweating. His body repelling the toxins in his bloodstream.

Darcy had rolled up his swag and was starting on

hers. "I'll pack up, then maybe you should drive him home."

"What about Molly?" Meghan asked as she gazed over at the horses nibbling at the weeds.

"I'll lead her home."

By the time the ute was packed, Lachie had stopped vomiting. Meghan helped him into the ute and rolled down the windows. Darcy gave her driving directions home and promised to see them soon. Meghan watched him through the mirror as she drove the ute away. It felt strange leaving him behind. Like she was leaving a little bit of her soul there by the creek. Back at the house, Meghan undressed Lachie and put him to bed. He needed to sleep off the hangover now that he had stopped throwing up. She pulled the sheets up under his chin and tiptoed out of the room. After showering and changing, she started down the hall. Darcy's bedroom door was open. Knowing he wasn't home yet, she cautiously stepped in and looked around.

Packed boxes lined the wall. Most of his belonging were gone. She sat down on his neatly made bed and gazed around the room. He really was moving out of the house. This had been his room since birth, and he was moving out so she could move in. Meghan felt guilty, but she reminded herself that she had said he could stay on. This was his decision. Besides he was a grown man, he should move out. This would be a good thing for him. Practice for when he bought his own station. Then he would be even farther away from the house. From her.

Even at the ringers' quarters, she could see him daily. He would check on the horses at least once a day, and she was bound to run into him in the paddocks. He would probably even come for dinner most nights.

A book on his bedside table caught her eye, and she touched it fleetingly. Lachie never read novels, and she wondered when Darcy had time to relax with a book. Despite being almost empty, the room still smelled like him. As though his scent had been absorbed into the paint and wooden frame. She stroked the pillow which still had an indentation where his head had been. Idly, she wondered what he dreamed about at night. Her heart skipped a beat. Did he ever dream of her?

Lachie felt better by midday and had eaten some toast then shut himself up in the office to work like always. Meghan had visited the horses and watched Moonshine walk around after his mother. Jasper and Molly were safety returned and happily grazing, but Darcy was nowhere to be seen, but there were many places he could be. Waterlines and troughs constantly needed to be maintained. Fences checked and repaired. There was always something for him to do. He had mentioned backburning some paddocks. She hoped he wasn't out there doing that now, alone. But glancing at the horizon, she didn't see any smoke clouds.

Finally, Darcy's ute pulled up at three in the afternoon, looking just as dusty and unkempt as its owner.

He was still in yesterday's clothes, with a day's worth of stubble growing. Meghan was sitting on the veranda folding towels, and she watched him walk up. He simply nodded in her direction after removing his dirty boots and went inside. Although her pulse quickened at the sight of him, she stayed quiet.

Fresh from showering and changing clothes he smelled a mite better than he had, when he sought her out later.

"Ready to go soon?" Darcy asked.

"Yep. I just need to grab my bag and say goodbye."

"Ten minutes then. I'll meet you at the ute."

Meghan nodded, and piled the towels into the basket and carried it inside.

She said goodbye to Lachie first who was hunched over books writing notes as he went, this was one place he could stay all day. He was so engrossed in whatever he was doing that when she called his name at first he didn't even hear her.

"I'm off then."

Lachie stood up hugged her. "Bye, sweetie. See you in a couple of weeks."

"I love you," she whispered more to herself than him.

"You too." He kissed her hair before pulling away and turning back to his work.

She paused for a moment, but he didn't look up so she left him alone.

Harriet hugged and kissed her and gave her a box of Anzac biscuits.

"Thank you," Meghan said, her melancholy lifting briefly. She was sad to be leaving. She was ready to be settled here and plan her future. It was what she wanted.

So why was she starting to doubt herself?

~

The first hour and a half of the flight back to Townsville was filled with polite conversation. Darcy was thoughtful and quiet while Meghan gazed out the window.

The image of smiling and relaxed Meghan wearing that skimpy bikini would be ineradicably burned in his memory long after she had left.

Something had shifted between them last night. Being so close to her in the moonlight he had the strongest desire to kiss her and he was sure she felt it too. She made him feel alive for the first time in years. How had he gone this long without feeling this way?

Now, instead of the easy conversation they were used to, nerves coursed through his veins and kept him silent. Scared he might not be able to stop himself from saying or doing something that he would come to regret. He resisted the urge to curse from his frustration.

He turned on the radio and they listened to the final strains of a country song. Meghan turned to Darcy with a knowing look when the familiar song from the night of the campdraft started.

When the song finally came to an end, Meghan turned to face him.

"Darcy. I need your honest answer on something?" Her voice quivered. "Can you give me any reason why I shouldn't marry your brother?"

Darcy's heart pounded in his chest. So many thoughts crossed his mind, so many crazy ideas and voices screaming in his head, but the only one he listened to was the one reminding him of his loyalty to Lachie.

He focused on the sky in front of him and shook his head slowly. "No."

He saw a flicker of disappointment cross her face before she turned back to the window, silent once more. The long flight seemed to be over too quickly. Before long Darcy landed the plane in Townsville, and he lowered the stairs for her.

"See you at the wedding," she called over her shoulder and rushed down the steps and away from the plane. Away from him.

Realization pounded in his heart. He wanted to call her back and tell her all the reasons he didn't want her to marry Lachie. He wanted to hold and kiss her, but all he could do was watch her walk away. If only he had met her first things would have been different, he would have told her how he felt a million times and not be ashamed to say it.

But, soon Meghan would be his sister-in-law. He had to accept that. It would be difficult to keep his feelings concealed if he saw her every day at the station. If she moved in, he would have to move out. Hopefully his feelings would fade over time.

He had a decent deposit saved, he decided to start looking for a station sooner rather than later. He would have to get away from Brigadier Station, and away from Meghan.

CHAPTER 11

The Strand along the city's foreshore was one of Meghan's favourite places; she often jogged along it after work, reflecting on her day and the things that had happened. She would also think about her mother. Would she be proud of her daughter? What would she think about these great life decisions she was making? Being in the city was different now, it felt as though she were seeing it through different eyes. There were people everywhere, in their cars, in the buses, jogging, cycling. On the ocean there were kite surfers, stand-up paddle boarders and tourists who ventured into the warm ocean, despite warning signs of recent crocodile sightings. The beaches were packed with kids playing in the sand. Today, Jodie had joined her for a brisk walk and Meghan was enjoying her companionship.

"Do you like Darcy?" Jodie asked her after hearing about her weekend.

"Of course I like him." Meghan grinned. "He's honest, loyal and fun. He doesn't play games like most guys do. And he cares. He has so much to offer someone." She couldn't help but smile as she thought fondly of the man who had come to mean so much to her in such a short time. "We have a lot in common."

"No, I mean like. You've talked more about Darcy than Lachie. Remember Lachie? Your fiancé." She teased but her eyes held a hint of concern.

"Yes, I remember Lachie." She paused wondering how to explain it. "The truth is I don't see much of him. He's always so busy."

"Too busy for you?"

"Well, yeah."

"No wonder you're lusting after Darcy then."

"I am not." Rubbing a weary hand across her brow, she turned to stare out at the ocean. She had dreamt about Darcy more than once, and if she was honest, he was on her mind more often than Lachie.

They walked in companionable silence for a few minutes thinking about her situation.

"Do you still love Lachie?" Jodie's eyes were bright with concern.

Meghan sighed. She wanted that life on the station: horses, cattle, chickens, mustering and drenching, rodeos and campdrafting... and a family. "Yes, I love him. Things are just tense right now, with the wedding. And the drought. Once it rains everything will be perfect."

"Then you need to focus on your fiancé."

"You're right. I said yes to Lachie. I promised him. I love him."

"Then marry him and be happy." Jodie bumped into her gently. "But promise to come and visit every now and then."

"Absolutely. We'll have an annual girls' weekend. Shopping and manicures."

"And cocktails." Jodie grinned brightly. "I'm going to miss you not being here."

Meghan pulled her friend close and they hugged. Tears welled in her eyes. Jodie's friendship meant a lot to Meghan, and she knew Jodie would always be there to support her. Arm in arm they turned to the ocean once more. The warm breeze danced along Meghan's face as she studied the hills of Magnetic Island, memorizing their rocky edges. She inhaled the salty air. It was so different from the dust they breathed on the farm. "I'll miss the ocean and the sand too."

Jodie squeezed her friend's arm. "It will always be here, waiting for you. Just like me."

～

Meghan stretched her stiff neck side to side. She couldn't wait to get there and walk around, her leg muscles were tight from the long drive. Even her eyes hurt from concentrating on the road.

Beside her, Jodie was still sleeping. She had the ability to sleep anywhere anytime which Meghan envied. Jodie had been excited and enthusiastic, despite the six-a.m. start. They had sung Bon Jovi songs and chatted animatedly all the way to Charters Towers. After a coffee and bathroom stop, the girls had felt refreshed. Then the scenery started looking the same, and the road stretched without any obvious landmarks lulling Jodie to sleep. It would be a long couple of days so Meghan let her sleep.

Tonight they would drive into Julia Creek and have dinner at the local pub. It was the only pub in town, and Friday was its busiest night. It hadn't taken much convincing from Harriet to get a group of friends to meet them there for a rehearsal dinner. Of course, most of those people would have to drive out to Brigadier Station the next day for the wedding, but they were all excited for a catch up and yarn and to see the most eligible bachelor in the district get hitched.

The mid-afternoon sun shone down harshly on the dry dusty paddocks as Meghan turned down the road that led to Harriet's house. It would always be Harriet's house, but my home Meghan thought as she caught sight of its green roof and the large ironbark trees behind it. She wound down the window and breathed in the humid spring air. Still no rain or clouds to be seen.

Jodie stretched and asked groggily if they were almost there.

"Welcome to Brigadier Station."

She sat up and looked around. "I expected a huge house, like in 'The Thorn Birds'," Jodie said disappointedly as she eyed up the modest house.

"The house is lovely and quaint. It's exactly what a family home should be." Meghan smiled. She loved the house and the history it held.

She parked her old Toyota Corolla in the driveway just as Harriet came out to meet them. She hugged Jodie as though they were old friends.

"This is Jodie, my best friend." Meghan introduced them.

"Lovely to meet you."

They gathered their belongings, which included three long, white dress bags. Jodie had to take the bags inside because Meghan was too short and they would have dragged in the dirt.

"Meghan's, mine and Lachie's suit," Jodie said as she double checked they were all there.

"You can put yours and Meghan's in Lachie's room. Oh sorry, I mean Meghan and Lachie's room." Harriet said as she pointed down the hall. "Lachie can take his to the ringers' quarters later. He'll sleep and change there with Darcy before the ceremony."

"So, Darcy's all moved out then?" Meghan peered into his old room. Only the furniture remained. All signs of the man who had lived there for twenty-seven years were all gone.

"Yes, he moved all his things out earlier this week. He's even looked at a station that's for sale." Harriet explained.

She knew it was coming, but that didn't prevent the sense of loss that rolled over her. Darcy wanted to move away. He was such a big part of Brigadier Station, it wouldn't be the same without him here.

"Is this where I'm sleeping then?" Jodie stepped into the room.

"Yes, it is. The bed has fresh sheets and the cupboards are empty for you." Harriet walked to the window and opened it, letting a fresh breeze blow in and carry away Darcy's familiar scent.

After freshening up, Meghan was eager to see the horses and go for a ride. She had missed them so much.

"Do you think Darcy would mind if I rode Jasper and Jodie rode Molly?" She asked Harriet.

"Those horses have been pining for you." Harriet smiled. "I don't think he'll mind."

Meghan nodded. She had secretly been yearning to ride the fine black horse that rode so well under Darcy's control.

Meghan expertly saddled the horses and gave Jodie a hard helmet to wear. Jodie immediately gave Meghan a questioning look. "Seriously, you know that will totally wreck my hair style?" she argued.

"Well, you getting brain damage if you fall off will ruin my wedding, so put it on." Meghan chided. Jodie sighed and did as Megan asked. Meghan put on her Akubra. The one Darcy had given her. "Why do you get to wear that?" Jodie asked folding her arms and raising her eyebrow.

"Because I have more experience than you do and besides there aren't any more helmets."

Using a stool, Jodie awkwardly mounted Molly and sat nervously in the saddle.

"Relax. Molly's a good girl." Meghan said as she stroked the mare's neck and kissed her affectionately. Then Meghan swiftly and expertly jumped onto Jasper's saddle.

Jasper turned to eye Meghan curiously. She stroked his neck in return. "It's okay boy. Darcy won't mind."

The horses slowly walked out of the stable. Molly followed Meghan obediently and soon Jodie relaxed into the movements. Meghan spotted Lachie's ute near the fence line so she directed the horses towards it.

When he came into sight Meghan looked admiringly over his broad shoulders, arm muscles flexing as he worked, fixing the fence. Then he heard the horses approach and looked up.

A storm of butterflies rose in Meghan's stomach as she recognized Darcy's profile and well, rounded jawline. He had grown a dark brown beard in her absence making him look mature and wise.

Darcy wiped his dirty hands on his jeans and lowered his hat, as they approached

"Hi." He smiled, but it didn't reach his eyes.

"Hi," Jodie said flirtatiously.

"I thought you were Lachie. Isn't this his ute?" Meghan pointed out.

"Yep. Mine's broken down, and I haven't had a chance to look at it yet." Darcy explained. "Lachie's on the quad, I think he's checking the drains."

"Exciting day tomorrow?" Jodie said breaking the

tension that was building between the two. "It'll be nice to see all you cowboys in suits."

"Can't say we have much use for suits out here." He turned his face up to the sun, and Meghan noticed a bruise near his eye that had been shaded by his hat.

"What happened to you?"

"Oh, it's nothing. I just got distracted." Darcy brushed off her concern. "I'm surprised Jasper let you ride him." He stroked his horse's long head.

"He didn't protest at all," Jodie said walking Molly closer to Darcy.

"Better get back to the fence." Darcy looked up at Meghan and their gaze held for a moment before he looked away.

"Enjoy your ride," he called to Jodie as he turned his attention back to the fence.

Jodie turned her horse, and Meghan pulled Jasper alongside.

She couldn't help glancing back over her shoulder but Darcy was hard at work, his hat sheltering his face from her view.

"Ready for a canter?" Meghan kicked Jasper gently and off they sped. Molly followed eagerly with Jodie holding on for dear life.

The main street was deserted except for the dusty trucks with bull bars on the front and dozing dogs in the back.

Inside the pub was packed full of family friends chatting, drinking and catching up on the local gossip. A local band was playing country music. Jodie was comfortable in any crowd and even though she didn't have much in common with the locals, she still made herself the life of the party. Meghan followed Lachie around and met his friends from school. They were nice enough but held the same reckless, mischievousness about them that Lachie had. Spotting Maddie and Dylan, she waved and joined them. These were her type of people. Honest and trustworthy.

"How are you? Excited?" Maddie asked after a hug.

"Well, to be honest, I'm very nervous," Meghan replied

Maddie grinned. "I guess it happens to everybody. I was a nervous wreck before my wedding. But then I saw Dylan as I walked up the isle and all the nerves fell away. I was marrying my best friend and the man I loved more than anything. That was all the confidence I needed." They gazed lovingly into each other's eyes.

Meghan smiled and sipped her wine as her heart skipped a beat. Was Lachie really her best friend? Would she feel the same kind of relief?

She found her gaze drifting to Darcy. He sat on a stool not far from Lachie. He was talking to Frank, the hardware store owner. Darcy looked very handsome tonight with a clean white shirt tucked into his jeans. He caught her staring and his jaw tightened before he turned away.

Soon people gathered, meals were ordered, and

more drinks were consumed. Lachie was never without a beer in hand and she noticed his words starting to slur after dessert.

With a long drive ahead, people started leaving. Everyone was excited about the wedding the next day and wished them happiness.

Harriet and Jodie waited in the car while Meghan said goodnight to her fiancé. He tasted like beer and the smoky aura made her cough.

"You'll be okay?"

"Yeah. Darcy will take care of me. Like always." They looked over as Darcy approached, sober and subdued.

"I'll see you both tomorrow then." Her hands shook as she turned and walked to the car. She glanced back before climbing in. Both men stood together watching the car full of women.

"Love you," she mouthed. As they drove away, she realised she had been looking at Darcy when she said it.

The ceiling fan whirled around at top speed sucking up the hot, humid air and pushing a slightly cooler breeze down on Meghan. Scantily clad in a pink cotton singlet and pink checked boxer shorts, the sheets were thrown off, she was still sweating and uncomfortable. It was more than just the heat and humidity, though. The evening's events kept playing over in Meghan's head.

Finally, giving up on sleep, she got out of bed and padded quietly to the kitchen where she poured herself a glass of cold water. It's just nerves, she told herself. Once she saw Lachie, everything would be fine.

Needing some fresh air, she pushed open the door and walked into the garden. Everything looked so beautiful and the smell of the roses was hypnotic. Harriet had been hard at work wanting to make everything perfect.

The smooth bristles of a dog brushed her leg and she looked down to see Joey staring back up at her. The dog was wide-eyed, and her tongue flopped to one side.

"Hello, mate. Can't you sleep either?" Meghan crouched down and stroked her, finding comfort in the dog's presence. Tears stung her eyes.

"Joey?" Darcy's timbre voice interrupted the otherwise peaceful night. Meghan looked over to find him walking up the path from the stables. Banjo at his heels.

Joey's attention flicked briefly to his master before returning to Meghan.

Meghan took in Darcy's appearance as he walked closer. He was wearing nothing but his old jeans. Her breath caught as her gaze lingered over his bare-chest and flat stomach.

"Can't sleep?" he asked.

"Too hot." With the back of her hand, she wiped at the droplets of sweat on her forehead.

"Yeah, that's the clouds," he pointed up at the dark night sky, "traps the heat in."

"Clouds mean rain," Meghan said hopefully looking at the sky.

"It would be a shame for it to rain on your wedding, though."

Meghan could see the affection in his eyes and had to fight every instinct in her body not to touch him. She searched for something to say. "Is Lachie alright?"

"Yeah, he's sleeping it off. He'll be fine by morning."

Meghan shifted uncomfortably. "I noticed he likes to drink. A lot."

His jaw tensed. "The problem is that when he starts he doesn't know when to stop. Just like Dad."

Meghan nodded. Lachie's dependence on alcohol had become increasingly obvious.

"You're free to do what you want, but make sure you marry the right man. For who he is, not what you want him to be." He reached out and brushed a stray hair from her face.

She closed her eyes at his touch, her body yearning for more. But, when she opened her eyes again, Darcy and the dogs were gone, and she was left wondering if it had all been a dream.

CHAPTER 12

*S*oft music played through Jodie's iPod as she styled Meghan's hair, teasing and pinning it in a chic up-do. Meghan studied her reflection in the mirror. The dark circles from a sleepless night were now concealed with foundation, her eyes were lined and shaded. Her lips were perfectly lined and painted in a rose-pink tone.

Meghan imagined herself as a mannequin being painted and dressed. As though she were seeing the scene but was not part of it. Jodie kept up an excited commentary of the night before about the people she had met and who she hoped to meet again. Meghan agreed and smiled where appropriate, but only vaguely listened.

"Meghan, I said I love your bracelet!" Jodie said jolting her back to reality.

She looked up at Jodie's reflection in the mirror as she nodded towards Meghan's right hand. On her wrist hung a delicate, gold, charm bracelet.

Meghan fingered it gently. "My dad gave it to my Mum when I was born."

"What are the charms?"

"There are only two. A heart and a horse. I don't know why she never added more." Meghan gazed at the two charms that sat side by side. The heart was curved and solid gold while the horse was intricately crafted. Looking at it reminded her of Darcy and their shared love of horses.

A sudden pain stabbed at Meghan's heart, and she clutched at her chest.

"Are you okay?" Jodie asked, worry in her voice.

"Could you get me some water?" she gasped.

"Of course." Jodie put down the comb and hurried out of the room.

The feeling eased and, alone for the first time that morning, Meghan stood and wrapped her dressing gown firmly around herself before walking to the window. Pulling back the curtains, she looked out over the sunburnt paddocks. The dark clouds in the sky threw shadows over the fields; the promise of rain could be smelt in the humid air that threatened to choke Meghan. She turned and looked at her delicate ivory dress hanging on the curtain rod. Her fingertips lightly stroked against the smooth satin. Her gold bracelet contrasted against the pale fabric.

Her thoughts turned to her mother. She wished she was there. Helping her get ready and giving her advice.

"I wish you were here, Mum," she whispered and

closed her eyes to the threatening tears. "I don't know what to do!" she admitted and fell to her knees, submitting to her emotions and letting tears stream down her cheeks while she gasped between her sobs. "I'm so confused, Mum. Please help me."

Jodie came in with a glass of water but quickly put it on the table when she saw her friend on the floor crying. She sat beside her and cradled Meghan against her chest.

"Are you alright? What can I do?"

Meghan tried to gain control of her tears when, suddenly, the fog of confusion lifted and only one thought was absolutely clear.

Don't do it. Don't marry him.

As if Mum had come to whisper into her ear. A sudden calmness came over her, and the tears slowed.

"I can't marry Lachie," she whispered, and then repeated it louder and with absolute conviction. "I can't marry Lachie."

"What? Why can't you? You're just nervous. It will pass." Jodie watched in shock as Meghan climbed to her feet and started shuffling through drawers looking for clothes to wear.

"No, it's not nerves. I can't marry him." She dressed quickly in jeans and a T-shirt. In a trance-like state she collected her belongings and threw them in her suitcase.

Jodie grabbed her by the shoulders, shaking her gently until her eyes lifted to look at Jodie. "Are you sure you want to do this?"

"Yes, I'm sure," Meghan declared with no reservations. "Please, get me out of here?"

Jodie nodded, released her and helped gather their belongings.

Bags packed, Meghan picked up her mobile and dialled Lachie, ready to apologize. She didn't want to see him even though she knew she should tell him in person. She just wanted to leave. Now.

The call went straight to message bank.

"I'm so sorry, Lachie... goodbye." Was all she could say before hanging up.

In their hurry to leave, Meghan bumped into Harriet in the hall.

"Meghan, what's wrong? What are you doing?" Harriet eyed up the luggage.

"I'm so, so sorry." Fresh tears, smudged with makeup slid from Meghan's eyes. "I know it's the worst thing I could do, but I can't marry Lachie. I called him to explain, but his phone is off."

Harriet pulled the young, emotional girl to her and hugged her reassuringly. "It's okay, sweetheart. You do what you have to do. I'll take care of everything here."

Meghan pulled back and frowned at Harriet. "How can you be so understanding? You put so much effort into this wedding, and I'm leaving him, at the altar." Meghan stifled a sob with her hand.

"Better you know now rather than later." Harriet held Meghan's hands in hers and looked deeply into her eyes. There was understanding there. Like Harriet knew exactly how she felt.

"Thank you," Meghan cried before hurrying to the car, Jodie close behind. She only allowed herself the briefest moment to take in the white plastic chairs and tables set up beside the rose bushes. Banjo raced over excitedly. She scooped him up and climbed into the passenger's seat.

"Everything will be okay," Jodie said as she started the car and drove away from the house.

Meghan watched out the dirty window as Brigadier Station slowly disappeared. A figure she thought might be Darcy stood outside the ringers' quarters. She didn't bother to ask Jodie to stop. There was nothing to say that would change anything now.

Droplets of water started to fall against the windows. Lightly at first, then faster and harder until the heavens opened up and rain thundered down on the hard, thirsty ground.

"Crap day for a wedding anyway." Jodie turned on the windscreen wipers.

Meghan sighed before closing her eyes, unable to watch the beautiful landscape any longer. Instead she focused on the sound the beating rain made against the car.

The rain had finally come. Just in time to wash away her dreams.

CHAPTER 13

*J*asper whinnied as he waited impatiently for Darcy to feed him.

"Hang on, mate." Darcy nudged him gently so he could pour the grain into the gelding's trough. He watched his faithful horse devour his dinner, having worked hard for it. Mustering was hot, hard work for the men who rode quads, let alone the ones who rode horses and the horses themselves. Jasper had earned his keep well and truly today, and Darcy had used some of his campdrafting techniques when rounding up the strays.

Darcy paused at Molly's stall and scratched her nose. Molly stamped her hoof into the dust.

"You miss her too?" he whispered.

"Darcy! Aren't you done yet?" Lachie called from the path leading between the house and stables. He was showered and freshly shaven already.

Darcy joined his brother and together they walked to the house as the sun created its nightly light show.

"You going out?" Darcy could smell Lachie's fancy aftershave. The expensive stuff he only wore when he was meeting a girl. He used to wear it for Meghan sometimes.

"Yeah, thought I'd hit the pub tonight." A hint of excitement in his voice. "It's been a while, gotta get back on the horse so to speak."

Darcy raised his eyebrows. Lachie had certainly made a swift recovery from his break-up with Meghan just one month ago. He had initially been upset and angry at Meghan leaving him at the altar without a proper announcement. He had seemed more embarrassed by the situation than truly sad that the woman he claimed to love didn't want to be with him anymore.

He never called her and barely spoke about her.

Lachie had played Meghan's voicemail to Darcy. His heart had ached at the sound of regret and pain she believed she was causing Lachie. He could hear the sadness in her voice and knew she had been crying before leaving that message.

Well, Lachie was never one to stay single... or rather celibate... for long.

If only it were so easy for Darcy to do same. It had taken him years to forget the pain Lisa had caused when she left him. Those wounds ran deep. It had taken him years to be able to trust again. It had taken Meghan's friendship to heal them. But when she left

Lachie, it felt like she had left him too, opening the scar back up and exposing it once more.

"Want to come? Leah and Emily might be there." Lachie grinned.

"Nah, I'm buggered and I've got an early start. Campdrafting in Richmond tomorrow." Darcy mentally made a list of things to pack for the weekend: swag, clean boots, toothbrush.

He was looking forward to a change of scenery. Brigadier Station had too many memories of Meghan's brief time here. The river, the garden, the house.

Harriet had expected him to move back in, but he was happy in the ringers' quarters, the only place where Meghan had not spent much time. At least not physically. She did haunt his dreams every night, though. Always there but never quite in reach.

"Good luck with the competition tomorrow. I'm sure you'll do great." Lachie slapped his back and hurried on ahead, eager to get to the pub. Had Meghan gotten over Lachie as easily? Was she already going out and meeting new people already?

Did she think of him as much as he thought of her?

$\sim$

The next day at the Richmond campdraft, Darcy and Jasper performed well in front of a large, cheering audience. Darcy waved to the audience when he collected his third-place prize. He found himself searching for Meghan's familiar face. She wasn't there of course. But he wanted her to be there. He wanted it so much. More than anything

Unable to sleep in his swag that night, Darcy decided to write Meghan a letter. He couldn't text her, that would be too impersonal, and he didn't have an email address. He found paper and pen and carefully considered how to start. At first, he thought of telling her how much he missed her, but he didn't want to come on too strongly. He had no idea of her feelings for him. Besides, she was Lachie's ex-fiancé, and that would never change.

It took a while before he found the right words.

Dear Meghan,

I'm at that Campdraft in Richmond. The one we were talking about. Jasper did brilliantly and we came third. You would have enjoyed it.

All the horses miss you, especially Molly. Moonshine is getting bigger every day.

Have you trained Banjo yet? Remember he needs lots of exercise.

I don't know why you left and I'm not asking for an explanation. I only want to let you know that I'm here. If you ever need a friend.

You are a beautiful person who deserves happiness and I wish you well.

Darcy

~

The chilled pink Moscato was refreshing and sweet, and Meghan drank deeply as she studied the painting set up on an easel in her living room. The outback scene she was working on looked finished, but Meghan felt something was missing. She dabbed at a spot with her paintbrush, then instantly regretted it.

"What does it need?" she murmured to herself.

"Meghan?" Jodie called out as she closed the front door. Jodie was a daily visitor now that Meghan was unemployed. Without her, Meghan fancied she would go for days without seeing anyone.

"Come to check if I'm still alive?" Meghan joked as Jodie came in. Despite the heat and humidity outside, Jodie still had a full face of caked-on makeup and perfect hair, unlike Meghan who was in a singlet with paint splashes and sweat stains. Her shorts were clinging to her damp thighs.

"I thought you might be out of wine!" She raised the shopping bag, and three wine bottles clinked together.

Meghan grinned. Good old Jodie. She had her priorities straight.

"Here's your mail." Jodie tossed a small pile of envelopes at her friend.

The first week after jilting Lachie she had gone into hiding in case he came after her. She didn't want to inflict any more pain on the poor man. But there had been silence.

Not a text message, not a call. Nothing for over a month.

Didn't he care at all? Didn't he want to know why

she had left him? Had he simply shrugged his shoulders and moved on? The fact he did not even want to speak to her made her feel even more assured she had done the right thing.

She put the paintbrush in the waiting cup of water and inspected the mail.

Bill, bill. Letter.

It was handwritten with no return address. Handwritten letters were rare these days. Her curiosity heightened she carefully opened it while Jodie rustled around in the kitchen.

"Darcy." His name slipped from her lips as her heart began to pound. She read the letter three times before Jodie returned.

"What's that?"

Meghan looked up still reeling from the shock of seeing his unpretentious handwriting in front of her. "It's from Darcy."

"Shit." Jodie snatched it from her hands and read it.

Meghan slumped down on the couch and finished off her wine in one large gulp. Darcy had been on her mind and in her dreams since she had left Brigadier Station. She had thought of him, even in her tears and foggy days. Memories of him still brought a smile to her face. She had often wondered if he was thinking about her or if he was angry at her for leaving his brother.

This is it. The answer she had been waiting for. She glanced at her wrist where the charm bracelet still hung. Reminding her of her own courage and strength.

"He's not angry," Jodie offered. "He misses you."

"Should I write back? What would I say?"

"Sorry, honey. I'm staying out of this one." Jodie handed back the letter. "They probably think I talked you out of the wedding and dragged you back to Townsville."

Meghan chewed on her lip. Darcy's words repeating in her mind: 'You are a beautiful person… if you need a friend.'

She missed his friendship, their easy conversation, and his warm, solid presence.

Jodie sat next to her on the couch and draped her arm across Meghan's shoulder. "Above all, you deserve love and happiness like he said, so listen to your heart. I'm sure your Mum would say the same thing too."

Meghan smiled weakly at her friend, tears stinging at her eyes. "Thank you," she said with a shaky voice. "For everything, thank you."

"You're welcome." Jodie hugged her. "I'll leave you to think about that. Call me if you need anything." Jodie gathered her things and waved from the door. "You two would make a cute couple, you know."

Meghan watched the door close before returning to the letter. She re-read it several times, imagining Darcy writing it. Perhaps he chewed on the pen as he chose his words. She closed her eyes and sighed. When she opened them her eyes fell upon the painting. She could almost feel the warmth of the sun as it set over the flat, scorched paddocks. She remembered the sunsets, the beautiful close of day. She closed her eyes again and

Darcy's face appeared in front of her. An easy smile on his face. His eyes filled with longing and passion. She felt herself lean forward to kiss him, but found only air. She covered her face and laughed at herself.

Knowing she would be too distracted to paint anymore she found some paper and a pen and sat at the coffee table.

"I don't actually have to send it," she told herself as she smoothed out the paper.

Dear Darcy,

Thanks for the letter. I appreciate your kind words and friendship. It has been a hard few weeks. Already I miss the dust and dry heat of the outback.

Summer has come, and it's humid and muggy here in Townsville. Not a rain cloud in sight, though.

Congratulations on your third-place win at Richmond. I wish I could have seen it. But I imagine you did a fantastic job as always.

Molly doesn't like to be left alone for long. Take her out an apple and spoil her. Girls like that. Tell her I miss her.

I miss you all.

Meghan.

She had lost more than just the man when she left Brigadier Station. She had lost the family who had welcomed her so warmly. The family she had wanted for such a long time. And friends who had promised her support and loyalty.

She could have had her heart's desire. But it would have been based on a lie. She was not in love with Lachie, and she doubted he was ever truly in love with her either.

Her heart was heavy with loss. She missed her mother and father, Harriet, and Darcy.

Especially Darcy.

Maybe they could be friends and exchange the occasional letter. They could never have anything more. Lachie would always be an unavoidable obstacle in their lives. He bound them together. Darcy knew this too. He asked for nothing more than friendship. That was all he wanted. It was all they could ever have.

CHAPTER 14

Sweat dripped down Darcy's back and soaked his khaki-coloured work shirt. He removed his Akubra and swiped the back of his hand across his moist forehead. The summer heat had arrived and, as predicted, was already reaching record highs. He searched the light blue sky. With no clouds in sight, it looked like the drought would continue another season. He replaced his hat and opened the wooden gate of the stable. Darcy patted each of the horses as he passed their stalls. Molly and Jasper were side by side and whinnying to each other as though in a secret conversation.

"What are you discussing today, huh?" Darcy scratched behind Molly's ear, she closed her eyes in reply. Jasper stepped forward and nudged Darcy's chest with his strong head, pushing Darcy back slightly.

"Whoa, trying to get rid of me, huh?" Darcy chuckled.

He squeezed past the horses and unravelled the hose next to the water trough. He turned it on and waited as water slowly pumped through. He watched the horses wander over and lower their heads, gulping down the warm artesian water.

The familiar ache returned to his chest as his thoughts turned towards Meghan. She was probably just waking up in her bed, he thought to himself. Had she dreamed of him as he had dreamed of her? Or would he be the first thing on her mind when she woke up?

He missed her face, her smile, her laughter, her easy conversation and her touch.

Her frequent, friendly letters were a comfort, but it wasn't the same as having her close by. Close to him. She had gotten her old job back and was resigned to continue her life as it had been before. She wasn't happy. He wanted to see her and be there for her.

He needed to see her.

If he saw her just one more time and said goodbye, he could stop torturing himself. His feelings for her had grown with every written conversation. Suddenly going to Townsville became the most important thing he had to do; he just had to see her before he went mad. He paused for a moment and thought about the day's jobs. Boar run wasn't due for another couple of days, and the fire breaks were done. Lachie could cover his chores for a day or two. If he flew down now, he could be back tonight.

Determined, he rolled up the hose, fed the horses and hurried back to the house to pack.

Within the hour, he had taxied the Cessna out of the hangar and was running through his pre-flight checklist.

Harriet and Lachie had happily sent him on his way after he had declared he urgently needed a new saddle and had to get it from Townsville. Harriet had given him a list of supplies she needed from a variety of shops, so Darcy had a good excuse to make the trip.

Darcy's hands shook slightly with nervous anticipation as he coaxed the aircraft off the ground and turned towards the coast. In just a few hours he would be walking in the city where she lived. Walking the same streets, she walked every day.

Would she be happy to see him? He hoped so.

Meghan sat under the air conditioner in the surgery's break room. She closed her eyes to the cool air blowing over her face. It reminded her of the winds which blew over the plains after sunset. She imagined herself back on the station, breathing in the smell of eucalypts and horse. Her heart tightened as she longed for those days again.

Despite knowing she had done the right thing by leaving, she still wished she could have stayed somehow. Instead, she was back working at her old job. In the old life she had wanted to escape.

A knock on her door startled Meghan and she looked up to see her boss, open the door.

"There's a man here to see you." Curiosity written all over her face.

"Me? Are you sure?" Meghan frowned, she didn't have any appointments booked.

The waiting room resembled the quietness of the day as the lone man stood with his back to her, facing the glass windows that separated him from the busy main road and footpath of the city.

She knew him from his broad shoulders and tapered waist. Her heart skipped a beat, and she moved her hands, one to her heart and one to her mouth as he turned his lean body to face her. He smiled nervously, his blue eyes bright and clear. Without hesitation, she flung herself at him and wrapped her arms around his waist, pressing her nose to his chest and breathing in his fresh country scent. She hadn't realised how much she missed him until she had him in her arms. He rested his chin on the top of her head. He felt so familiar and comfortable. She never wanted to let go.

"What are you doing here?" Meghan asked with her voice slightly muffled as she laid her cheek against the pocket of his clean work shirt.

"Had some jobs to do. Thought I'd see if you were free for lunch." They stood still, neither of them eager to break the embrace.

"I'd love to." She smiled up at him and gazed into the blue eyes that continued to haunt her thoughts and dreams. "I missed you."

"I missed you too," he admitted quietly. He held her gaze for a moment before lowering his eyes to her lips. Meghan's pulse quickened.

A dog barked in an examination room, breaking the moment. Darcy looked away as Meghan finally stepped out of his arms.

"I'll just grab my bag," she said as she stepped back and clumsily bumped into the coffee table.

"Are you okay?" He touched her arm as she regained her balance.

"I'll be back in a second." Recovering she smiled then turned and hurried off. "Just breathe," she told herself as she retrieved her handbag.

When she returned, he was holding the door open for her. "Ready?"

"I am." She beamed. Happier in this moment than she had been for months.

The café Meghan chose was situated on the tip of the Strand overlooking the ocean. The hostess seated them at a table separated only by a wire fence, from the rocky cliff and the sparkling water below.

Darcy took a moment to appreciate the view. He could clearly see the mountainous form of Magnetic Island and the various barges and boats on the channel.

"I can't remember the last time I saw the ocean, except from the air," Darcy explained when he caught Meghan's questioning gaze.

"Really? That long?" Meghan frowned.

"We had a family holiday in Cairns when we were still at school," he said with a smile. As good as the view was, it didn't compare to the view of Meghan sitting across from him, her long hair loose and free, caressing her bare arms. He was all too aware of their knees bumping under the table, and his heart pumping so loud he was sure Meghan could hear it.

The waitress came and took their drink orders. Darcy ordered a locally brewed beer to try, while Meghan opted for lemonade.

"It's so good to see you," Meghan said, as her hand briefly patted his forearm. "How is Harriet?"

Darcy leaned forward casually, eager to be as close as possible. "She's good. The CWA has her baking for an upcoming fundraiser. How's my mate, Banjo?"

"He's fine. Growing so big." She bit her lip and studied the salt and pepper shakers. "How's Lachie?"

"He's good. He goes into town a lot on weekends." He watched for Meghan's reaction not wanting to hurt her feelings, but still wanting to make it clear his brother had moved on.

"Is he seeing anyone?" She raised her eyes, and he searched them for signs of regret.

"He's not serious with anyone, but he is, um, getting out, if you know what I mean."

"So, he's moved on. Good for him."

Darcy watched a series of emotions cross her face, ending with relief and content.

"No wonder he didn't call for an explanation," she murmured.

"You don't regret it."

"We started out so real, but somewhere along the way we lost it. I think I lost a bit of myself too." Her thick lashes lifted. "I don't regret anything though, I just hated the way it ended. You were right, I was going to marry him for the wrong reasons. I would have regretted it."

"Honestly, I think Lachie was going to marry you for the wrong reasons too." Darcy gently took Meghan's right hand in both of his. He noted how small and fragile it looked in his large rough ones.

"Harriet must hate me so much."

"No. She could never hate you. I think she understands."

Meghan smiled. "He's lucky to have a family like you."

He realised just how lonely she was now without them. She had no one except Jodie in her life. No wonder she had been so eager to marry Lachie and become part of his family. He couldn't imagine not having his relatives close by. Meghan didn't have that. No one else alive remembered her childhood or her parents the way she did.

"Harriet misses you. You can call her anytime. She thinks of you as a daughter."

His arms twitched at the flicker of hope in Meghan's eyes. He wanted to hold her and tell her everything would be okay.

He opened his mouth to say something but was interrupted by the waitress bringing their drinks.

"How long are you in Townsville for?" Meghan asked after they had ordered their meals.

Darcy wanted to prolong his trip as long as possible. "At least until tomorrow. Mum gave me a list so I guess I'm going shopping this afternoon."

"You're welcome to stay at my house. I've got plenty of room," she suggested. "Jodie and I are going to see a band play in town tonight. You want to come?"

Darcy looked sceptical. "Do they play country music?"

"Not exactly, but it's good. I actually think you'd like it."

"Okay, sounds good, as long as I won't be cramping your style." She could have told him Britney Spears was playing and he still would have said yes. All he wanted was an opportunity to spend more time with her. He didn't care what they did.

"You won't be. I'll call Jodie to tell her you're joining us. She's bringing her new boyfriend so I would've been the third wheel. This way you can be my date." She blushed. "I mean, well, you know."

He smiled, pleased to see her reaction. "I'd love to be your date."

Darcy enjoyed their all-too-brief lunch, and before long they were back in front of the vet surgery.

"So, I'll see you later." She turned to say goodbye.

"I'm really looking forward to it." He stepped closer, touching distance. She moved into his hug. When she looked up at him, her eyes glowed with affection. Slowly he moved his head closer, the need to kiss her overpowering him.

He was so close he could feel her warm breath on his face.

"Excuse me." A middle-aged man with a cat cage waited impatiently pointing to the door which they were blocking.

"Sorry." Darcy released Meghan and stepped aside. His hands fell to his thighs, feeling empty without her warmth.

Meghan was leaning against the wall. She opened her mouth but before she could speak he put his finger against her lips. He didn't want to hear any regret or apology.

"I'll see you tonight," he whispered, a hint of possibility in his voice.

CHAPTER 15

"Friday nights are always pretty busy on Flinders Street," Meghan explained as they rode in the back seat of the taxi that evening. "Thanks for coming. I know it's not really your scene."

Darcy was all too aware of Meghan's bare knee against his. Her tight, black skirt had ridden halfway up her thigh in the twenty-minute car ride from her house to the city centre. Her pale shoulders were bare apart from thin straps of her purple top. The temptation to touch her skin and feel her warmth was almost too much to bare.

"It'll be fun." He grinned at her.

She pulled her hair away from her neck and exposed a rapidly beating pulse. He felt his own heartbeat hammer in time to it. He licked his lips, wanting nothing more than to run them over her long neck and taste her skin.

"They're a really good band, I promise."

He paid for the taxi when it stopped in front of the pub. She tried to give him money, but he refused. "You're letting me sleep on your couch, it's the least I can do."

Darcy led the way into the crowded bar, his warm hand placed gently on her lower back, guiding her through the throng of people. At the bar they ordered rum and cokes as they watched the band set up.

Jodie, swaggered over with a young, blond man with tattoos and a vacant expression.

"Hello." She smiled at Darcy before turning to Meghan with a wink.

"Hi, Jodie, how are you?" He shouted over the chatter of people.

"I was quite shocked that you were in Townsville and willing to come for the show. What brought you to town?"

"I just decided to stop by and check on you girls." Darcy wished he had better social skills for this kind of situation. He should have made more of an effort over the years rather than confining himself to the property.

"Well, it is good to see you. Oh, this is Ashton." The scruffy blond man offered a half-hearted handshake.

"Well, we're going to dance, so I'll catch you two later," Jodie said as the musicians warmed up. "By the way, you look good." Her eyes flitted between both him and Meghan and he couldn't quite figure out what she meant by the comment.

～

Meghan let the music flow through her body and swayed to the beat. Darcy swayed his hips to the beat confidently, not afraid to look silly. She admired his sexy swagger. Dressed in smart jeans and striped, collared shirt, he looked gorgeous. She noticed she was not the only one lusting after him. A group of girls across the room were trying to catch his eye.

Her stomach hardened at the thought of Darcy being with someone else. No man had ever sent her pulse racing like this. No one had touched her heart or stirred her senses till she could think of nothing else but how much she wanted him.

One taste of his lips, one touch of his skin was all she needed to know if this was just a romantic fantasy. Her heart was telling her that he wanted her just as much as she wanted him. Experimentally she started moving her hips more and stood a little closer to Darcy so their bodies touched lightly. His body responded. His hands hovered near her hips. His jaw was tense, and his eyelashes lowered.

A jostling of people next to him broke the spell and Darcy turned back to his drink. He took a mouthful before replacing it and glanced back to Meghan. She stood on tiptoes and leant against him to speak into his ear.

"Wanna get out of here?"

He took a second to think about it before nodding and motioned for her to lead the way. Humidity slammed into them like a rainstorm as they walked out of the noisy pub. Groups of twenty-year-olds lined the street talking to each other. Meghan pointed down a dimly lit road. "This one leads to the Marina." She started down the pathway.

"Are you sure? I thought you liked that band."

"I do, but I was getting claustrophobic in there with all those people." She would prefer his company tonight. Alone.

"Yeah," he agreed as he walked beside her, hands in his pockets. "I'm getting too old for that."

"We're not that old. We just prefer country entertainment." She bumped against him playfully.

ANZAC Park lay ahead of them, and they paused to watch the rounded concrete fountain as its water went through a cycle of rainbow colours. Above them, the stars twinkled beside the moon. Not quite as bright as on the plains, but a reminder that there were no clouds carrying rain.

The marina was full of yachts and catamarans. They watched the boats gently rock. The water lapped against them. The noise barely a whisper in the still night.

"I'm really glad you're here."

"I'm glad I came too. Though I probably shouldn't have." His eyes found hers, and she licked her dry lips. His gaze followed the action.

She wanted to kiss him. To see what it was like. People kissed all the time, it didn't need to change anything. Her body moved toward him as though it didn't need her approval. Before she could get too

close, Darcy placed his hands on her shoulders stopping her.

"We shouldn't." His face was tense, and he grimaced
slightly.

"I know," she murmured staring at his chest,
berating herself for being so brazen.

"I mean I want to. God. I really want to." He sighed.

"Me too," she whispered back. Even Meghan could
hear the pleading in her own voice.

His fingers gently stroked the sensitive skin on her
shoulders, sending shivers rippling through her body.
She closed her eyes to the sensation. Knowing it was all
she could have.

"Fuck it," he said, a moment before his lips claimed
hers.

He wanted to take it slowly. If this was the only kiss
they ever shared it had to be memorable. He slipped his
arms around her and her skin was soft and smooth
beneath his palms. Her curves nestled against him. The
perfect companion for his body. She was soft and
warm and womanly, and his desire grew so fierce he
could barely breathe. His lips moved over her mouth
slowly, back and forth. She tasted like strawberry and
smelled of fruity soap. He wanted to taste her body to
see if it all tasted like fruit, or something even better.

Meghan moaned softly and tightened her grip
around his hips, pushing herself against his groin.

Helpless and unbearably aroused, his plan for restraint was forgotten as his kisses were fuelled by a fierce hunger. He ravaged her soft mouth with his tongue but she responded, matching his need, clinging to him.

He'd never felt such desire before. It was like a dream, yet so real. The intoxicating sweetness of her mouth and the warmth radiating off her body left him in an utter state of wantonness. Her hands started groping at his clothes and pulled his shirt free from his jeans. Her small hands crept up his chest, tugging the shirt up with them. He swallowed a moan as her fingers brushed his nipples and almost pushed him over the edge.

A bird chirped overhead reminding them they were in a public place. He broke away and bent to kiss her hands. Her eyelids were heavy, and she was panting. He held her close as he regained his composure.

He brushed her hair from her face. "Let's get a taxi."

"Okay." Her voice was husky with need. "Take me home."

Darcy's hands itched to touch her. His body burned with desire. But he didn't dare even hold her hand, knowing that once he started, he wouldn't be able to stop. He had never felt more vulnerable in his life. The barriers he had so carefully built around himself were just a pile of dust now. His thoughts were entirely centred on Meghan. His senses were heightened to everything about her. Her sweet smell. Her slightest move. He could even hear every breath she took. His own breathing fell into the same rhythm so it seemed they were breathing as one. His stolen gazes would take in just a portion of her. Her slender legs moving from side to side, jostled by the movement of the car. Her hands clutched tightly in her lap. Her hair, damp from the humid evening, sticking against her neck. Her chest, rising and falling with each breath.

By the time the taxi pulled up in front of her house he was a mass of pent-up desire on the verge of release. He pushed notes into the driver's hand and scrambled out of the vehicle. She was unlocking the front door. He caught up to her as she crossed the threshold and he closed the door behind him.

He leaned against the wall opposite as he watched her.

"Meghan." Darcy finally broke the silence. "I can't stay away from you anymore."

She took a sharp breath and bit her lip. "I don't want you to." She took a careful step towards him. "I want you, Darcy." Her voice was deep and full of longing.

One step closer and their shirts brushed, her nipples hardening against him. Her head fell to the side exposing the side of her neck, offering it to him.

He accepted it without hesitation. His warm breath gently caressing her sensitive skin. His lips pressing gentle kisses on her as his hands glided up her arms and pulled her closer to him. She raised herself onto tiptoes and pressed her hungry lips against his. It was a kiss beyond wonderful, deep and ardent, breathtaking in its sensual promise. But it was not enough. His fingers threaded through her loose hair, the other hand at her back pressing her closer towards his body. Their lips and tongues explored each other hungrily. She ran her hands up his hips and back feeling his hard muscles. He kissed her again, lifting her up off the floor this time. Meghan wrapped her legs around his waist as he carried her down the hall. When he found her bedroom, he knew this was the point of no return. Once they crossed the threshold they would be altering the course of their lives.

She kissed away his apprehension. This was exactly what he wanted to be doing. Consequences be damned.

He laid her down on the pale sheets, noting the contrast against her dark hair as it tumbled around her. "You are so beautiful."

He was fascinated by her blush he wondered if it was because she rarely received compliments or because he'd given it.

She reached for the buttons on his shirt, and he obliged by tearing it off and throwing it behind him. With his chest exposed to her seductive scrutiny, he felt himself harden even more. It was almost unbearable now. He wanted to take it slow, to enjoy every sensation, but his lust was barely contained, and he didn't think he could hold back much longer.

She raised herself and tugged at her top, exposing skin that never saw the sun. He kissed her lightly just below her ribs, and she giggled.

"Are you ticklish?"

"Just a little bit. Sometimes." She grinned. "Are you?"

Before he could answer, she patted her fingers

lightly over his sides. He squirmed and tickled her back until he was forced onto his back and she straddled him. She caught his hands and held them above his head. Then with deft fingers removed her shirt uncovering her plump breasts. His eyes widened as he took in their brown peaks. He moved his hands to cover their weight and she leaned into him. Her lips claimed his. Her tongue explored his mouth with quick flicks.

Her greedy hands moved between them and easily freed him from his jeans, sliding them from his body. She stood and shimmied out of her skirt and underwear. Darcy let out an audible gasp as he took in her naked body. She was the most stunning woman he had ever seen.

He sat on the edge of the bed and reached for her hand. She gave it to him and he gently kissed her knuckles. "It's been a while since I've been with a woman," he admitted, vulnerable in every way.

"I know," she replied stepping closer and stroking his head. "I'll try to be gentle."

He smiled slyly at her comment. "No, don't do that."

She licked her lips and pushed him back against the bed. Kissing his chest and abdomen as she went lower. He moaned loudly as her mouth circled him and had to reign himself in. When he felt ready to burst, he pulled her up and she straddled him again, taking him deep inside her and rocking against him. It didn't take long until they were both panting and breathless. Together they tumbled over the edge, clinging to each other as they came down.

"Wow." He sighed as he pulled her back against him, spooning her from behind.

"Oh yeah." She snuggled into him.

Darcy fell into a fitful slumber his arms wrapped around Meghan with no desire to ever let her go.

CHAPTER 16

*M*oonlight streamed through the windows and the air conditioner hummed; it was the only thing that broke the silence of the night. When Darcy opened his eyes the first thing he saw was Meghan's peaceful face, her eyes closed, still fast asleep. Her head rested on his shoulder, her arm was draped across his abdomen.

Darcy reached down with his free hand and pulled the sheet further up over them so she wouldn't get cold. She was so beautiful and so sexy even in her sleep. Last night had not only been incredible but magical. He had never felt so connected to a woman. Last night had felt like their souls connected.

He wondered if it had been as powerful for her. How could it not have been? Then Lachie slipped into his thoughts, not of guilt but of worry. How did his performance compare to his brother's? Lachie had more experience and was more experimental than him.

He knew sex wasn't everything, but he understood that it was a vital part of a relationship. Lachie was ahead of him when it came to women.

How would Lachie react if he found out they had slept together? It felt so right, so natural for him to be with her. How could it be wrong? Surely Lachie would understand in time. Wouldn't he?

Meghan's hand brushed teasingly across his chest.

"Hi." Her voice was husky from sleep.

Darcy looked down and grinned at her happy, satisfied smile. All thoughts of Lachie evaporated, his attention and thoughts solely on the gorgeous woman in his arms.

Darcy entwined his fingers with Meghan's and kissed her hand.

She raised herself up on her elbow and looked Darcy in the eye.

"No regrets?" Her voice quivered slightly.

"Hell no… no regrets at all," he replied and kissed away her worries.

She placed her soft hand against his stubbly cheek. "I want this to be the beginning of something, Darcy. Tell me how you feel and please don't play with my heart."

Relief swept over him like a wave. He hadn't misinterpreted her affections, she felt this too. "I've never lied to you, Meghan, but I have lied to myself. I told myself I could suppress my feelings for you. That I didn't love you." He stroked her hair tenderly. "I'm real glad you didn't marry Lachie. I'm so bloody in love with you."

Her eyes watered. "I'm in love with you too. There could never be anyone else."

His arms enveloped her and their mouths came together again. They made love slowly and passionately, proving their powerful feelings for each other over and over again as the moon descended and the sun took its place.

~

"Not too much further," Meghan called encouragingly a couple of meters up the rocky mountain incline.

"People do this every day?" Darcy paused and bent over, hands on his knees, while he caught his breath. He was used to doing strenuous work on the station but the 'Goat Track' walk up Castle Hill was a serious workout.

"It's a rite of passage in Townsville. If you can conquer Castle Hill, you can do anything!" Meghan said. She admired Darcy's form as she watched him rest. His skin flushed from exercise, rivers of sweat trickling from his body staining his new blue singlet. His black shorts exposed tight calves and thighs, so rarely exposed to the elements. His body was now as familiar to Meghan as her own after their four amazing weekends together. They were into a routine now, he flew down late Friday night, and she collected him from the airport. They spent all night and most of the next morning making up for the time apart, before heading out for lunch and sightseeing.

She had introduced him to art galleries, plays and real barista-made coffee. He had been intrigued and receptive to all the new experiences city life offered.

"Can we take the road down?" Darcy asked before drinking deeply from his water bottle.

"Of course, the Goat Track is better going up than down." The rocky steps and loose gravel made it difficult and hard to manoeuvre in places. "I promise it will be worth it at the top."

Ten minutes of steep stairs later, they reached the top and were welcomed by the magnificent view of Townsville and Magnetic Island. His eyes widened as he took in the view.

Despite the humidity and scorching November sun, there were many people at the lookout taking in the remarkable view.

"So, we could have driven." He grinned as he waited for a car to pass by, hoping to find a vacant parking space.

"Yeah, but that would be cheating." She stepped closer and wiped away the sweat from his face with her towel before kissing him softly. "Well done."

Darcy enveloped her in his arms. "I'm glad to see you're not exhausted. You'll need your energy for later." He teased as he returned her kiss.

Meghan held him tightly. Her love for him had grown more every day. How had she not seen how perfect they were for each other from the start?

"Darcy." Meghan started shyly. "I miss you so much when you're not here. It's getting harder to let you go. What are we going to do?"

He exhaled. "I know. I guess I could move to Townsville."

"You'd do that?" She was surprised by his reply.

"I'd do anything for you."

Meghan considered a future in the city with Darcy. What would he do? Jobs were scarce since the mining collapse, and his talents were better spent in the country. "You belong on a station. We belong on a station. I'm concerned about your family. How are we going to tell Lachie?" She voiced the worry that had haunted her all these weeks. He would have to be told. But how? How could they break such overwhelming news and not have their betrayal tear the family apart?

"He's already clued on that I'm seeing someone here," Darcy explained. "Lachie keeps grilling me for more information."

"What do you say?"

"I tell him to piss off, that it's none of his business." Darcy nuzzled her neck. "I will tell him but the time's not right. Not yet."

"Alright. But we can't let it go too long. Lying about it will add to the betrayal." Her words were wise. She had thought long and hard about it.

She turned to him with a gleam in her eye. "Have you got your mobile?"

"Yeah." Darcy pulled it out of his pocket. His phone

was getting some serious use now with their daily phone calls and frequent text messages.

She took it and positioned it to take a selfie of them. The first photo she took they were both smiling blissfully, like they didn't have a care in the world. Then she set it up again, but this time, they were kissing when they took the photo. Their love for each other captured forever.

CHAPTER 17

*D*arcy swatted at the flies swarming around his face and sucked in a hot, dusty breath as he watched the Droughtmaster cattle push their way into the mustering yards, lowing noisily. He whistled Joey to keep the mob tight as he and Lachie took up the rear.

"That's it." Lachie called as the last cattle finally pushed through the gate and he latched it in place.

Lachie strode over to his brother. "I need a beer. Still some in the ringers' fridge?"

"Sure is." Darcy answered as they fell in step and walked to the fibro building Darcy was still calling home. He liked his new-found privacy and it meant he could talk to Meghan on the phone without worry that someone might overhear.

He removed his Akubra and wiped his forehead with his shirt sleeve as Lachie pulled two cold beers from the fridge.

The sun was setting behind the yards as the men sat at the table and nursed their beers. Lachie made quick work of his and retrieved another one before Darcy was even half way through his.

"What time is the truck coming tomorrow for the heifers?" Darcy asked.

"Noon. Plenty of time to sort them." Lachie answered and stretched his long legs out. "You around this weekend or playing hookie with your girl?" he teased.

"Staying here. Too much work to do." Darcy was sick of Lachie's teasing and he still wasn't sure how to tell him about Meghan.

As if on cue his mobile started ringing. He reached for it quickly in his back pocket and silenced it. Meghan's picture disappeared as the phone darkened. He placed it on the table and lifted his beer to his mouth. She'd understand when he called her back and explained why he couldn't take her call.

"Have you still got Dad's stock whip?" Lachie eyed him curiously. "Thought I might try my hand at it."

"It's in the shed." Darcy nodded in the direction of the shed next to the ringers' quarters.

"Can you grab it? I can never find anything in there."

Darcy pushed back from the table and did as his brother asked.

It took a while of sorting through boxes and dust to locate the whip and when Darcy finally returned with it, he found Lachie next to the fridge, red faced as he scrolled through Darcy's phone.

"Shit!" Darcy muttered under his breath, rebuking himself for carelessly leaving the phone on the table. Meghan had tried to lock it with a password but Darcy had stopped her from complicating the blasted thing.

Lachie would have been eager to see what this elusive girlfriend looked like and what romantic texts were being exchanged. Now he had his answer and he didn't like it.

"Meghan?" Lachie looked up and showed his brother the picture of Meghan and Darcy kissing. "Of all bloody people, you're screwing my ex-fiancé?"

Darcy took a slow step toward him, arms raised the way he would approach a spooked horse.

"It only started after she went back to Townsville."

Lachie finished his beer and pulled out another, sculling it like water.

"Hey, slow down, mate," Darcy said tersely.

"You shut up and don't tell me what to do," Lachie yelled furiously. "I was going to marry her! Is that why she left? She chose you instead?" His voice dripped with disgust and hatred.

Lachie threw the phone on the concrete floor in front of Darcy. The impact caused the phone to break apart.

"I swear we were just friends then. I—"

"Shut up. I don't want to hear any of it. You bastard!" Lachie launched himself at Darcy and started pounding him with his fists.

Usually Darcy was the underdog when they wrestled, and although Lachie's fist collided painfully on his cheek and ribs, his aim was marred by his intoxication. Lachie winded him in the stomach and took the opportunity to move back a few steps.

"I'm sorry. We never wanted to hurt you, believe me," Darcy said as he wiped blood from his cheek.

Lachie held his stomach and panted for a few minutes before looking back up at his brother. "Fuck you, Darcy, and get off my property."

Darcy stared at him but stood his ground.

"Fuck you both." Lachie screamed and limped out of the ringers' quarters.

Darcy bent down and retrieved the pieces of his broken phone.

For better or worse the truth was out. Darcy would try talking to him again tomorrow. When he was sober.

He heard the rough noise of a motor starting and he lifted his head to see Lachie sitting on his quad bike starting it up in the darkness. What was the fool doing? He asked himself.

Darcy rushed out to stop him but the bike was already speeding off into the night. "Lachie!" he screamed.

A few seconds later a chilling, smashing sound echoed through the paddocks, followed by an explosion of flames.

～

The flames were spreading rapidly, their red tongues spitting embers to neighbouring dry grass. Darcy was engulfed in fear as he saw the smoke rise to the sky. He screamed Lachie's name as he ran towards the accident.

He found Lachie's limp body far enough from the fire and wreckage of his quad bike to assume he had been thrown when the bike hit the old gum tree. The fuel tank had probably exploded.

Darcy checked his brother's neck for a pulse. He felt it faintly under his fingers. By the firelight, he could see his chest was rising slowly but his neck looked to be at an awkward angle.

His own heart racing, fearing for his brother's life, Darcy rummaged for Lachie's cell phone in his pants. "Lachie stay with me," he whispered as he searched for the phone. Once retrieved, he scrolled through his contacts and found the number for The Royal Flying Doctor Service.

As he relayed information to them, two minutes later he saw headlights approaching the scene. Darcy ended the call as Harriet ran to Lachie's side.

"The RFD is sending in the helicopter in case it's a spinal injury." Darcy told his mother as she knelt beside her eldest son. "They said not to move him."

Silent tears slid down her cheeks as she placed her hand on Lachie's chest to monitor his breathing.

"I'll stay with him. You need to deal with that." Harriet pointed to the fire.

The flames were struggling to find nourishment in

the sparse, dry grass, the gum tree now fully emblazed. Darcy felt its warming heat and watched the broken remains of the quad bike melt.

Darcy checked Lachie's pulse again. "I'll take your car and get the extinguisher." He said and passed the mobile to his mother. "You take this in case anything changes."

Darcy climbed in his mother's Land Cruiser and drove quickly back to the ringers' quarters. As he parked the car he hit the steering wheel in anger, "Shit, shit, shit!" He screamed. His eyes stung from the smoke. He could smell it on his clothes.

Stupid Lachie, riding that thing in the dark, drunk and angry. Stupid me, for not stopping him.

CHAPTER 18

*M*eghan glanced at the time on her mobile. Why hadn't Darcy called her back yet? He always called at this time of day. She imagined him, clean and fresh from his evening shower. His hair dampening his neck. A warm, tingly sensation spread through her body at the thought of him. He was a passionate man who could be surprisingly gentle. Her appetite for him never seemed to be sated. The more she got the more she wanted. Their separation was driving her crazy with desire. It had only been three days since his last visit, but already she was aching to see him again.

The familiar ringtone came from her mobile and she reached for it excitedly, but stopped when she saw Lachie's number displayed. Her heart raced and she debated not answering it. But what if Darcy was using his brother's phone? Although that didn't seem likely considering they were keeping their relationship secret until Darcy found the right time to tell him.

What if Lachie had found out? He could be calling to confront her. Only one way to find out.

"Hello." Her voice was nervously quiet.

"Meghan. It's Harriet."

"Harriet. Hi, how are you?" Meghan relaxed into the sofa. It was comforting to hear the older woman's voice.

"I'm at the Townsville Base Hospital. There's been an accident." Harriet's voice was choked with emotion.

Cold panic swept through Meghan like a flash flood. "Is it Darcy? Is he okay?"

"Darcy's fine. He's flying here now. It's Lachie, he's in surgery."

Meghan swallowed hard. Panic setting in. He must be in bad condition to be airlifted to Townsville. "Oh, my God. What happened?"

"Darcy said he drove his quad bike into a tree. He'd been drinking. The doctors suspected spinal injuries so he was helicoptered here instead of Mt Isa. I flew here with him."

"I'm leaving now. I'll be there soon." Meghan knew how it felt to wait for a loved one to come out of emergency. She knew Harriet wouldn't want to be there alone. She didn't need to ask.

"Thank you."

After she hung up the phone her mind whirled with possibilities. Why did he drive his quad bike into a tree? What if he died?

She gathered her bag and keys and looked around the room, shock over taking her.

"Please Lachie, don't die."

~

The emergency department was freezing cold after the heat of the night outside and Meghan shivered as she strode through the heavily disinfected corridor. She knew exactly where Harriet would be. Grief for her own mother piled on top of her as she remembered the helpless, terrified agony of waiting to hear the outcome of emergency surgery. She braced herself against a bleached white wall while waves of fear washed over her. Not again please. Please God, don't let him die here too.

After a few deep breaths, she continued her path and soon came upon the waiting room. There she was. Harriet sat, head down, her greying hair fell like a curtain around her face.

Harriet looked up as Meghan approached. Ridged with tension she stood and accepted Meghan's comforting embrace.

"Have you heard anything?" Meghan noted the dark circles around Harriet's eyes.

"Nothing yet." Harriet shook her head and fell back into the hard plastic chair as though her knees had buckled.

Meghan held her friend's hand. "What happened?"

"Darcy said they argued and Lachie drove off on the quad. It crashed into a tree and exploded."

"Oh, my God." Meghan put her hand to her mouth. She imagined the scene and thought of how horrifying it must have been for Darcy to witness the event.

A doctor dressed in blue scrubs approached. "Mrs. McGuire."

Meghan was swamped with grief, she looked at Harriet whose eyes mirrored her fear.

"Yes. How is Lachie?"

"We've successfully stopped the bleeding and we're waiting for some test results. He's bruised substantially and has two broken ribs, suspected nerve damage in his arm and legs and some minor burns."

"Will he be okay?" she begged.

"He's in a coma. We'll know more when he wakes up." The doctor put his hand on Harriet's shoulder. "He's young and strong. The sooner he wakes up the better."

Harriet slumped against Meghan who put a supportive arm around her. "Can we see him?"

"Sure. Come this way." The Doctor lead them to the intensive care ward. It was cold and filled with people in various casts and bandages.

Behind a curtain, they were shown Lachie's bruised and bloodied body. Bile rose in Meghan's throat while Harriet sobbed at the sight of her son. There was a cannula in his arm pumping lifesaving blood and saline back into his body.

Harriet sat in a chair and held his free hand. She spoke soft words of comfort to her son.

Tears flooded down Meghan's face and she covered her mouth to muffle her sobs. His skin was so pale. Like he was dead. He still might die. He might not wake up. If he does he might have severe brain injuries. Until he woke up no one knew for sure what the extent of his injuries would be. Lachie was so young, with so much living still to do. This couldn't be happening to him. It wasn't fair. She squeezed her eyes shut but a memory of her mother's broken body lying in a similar hospital bed invaded her thoughts. Her mother had never regained consciousness after the accident. Meghan had never been able to say good bye. To tell her she loved her.

She swallowed past the sadness that remained as raw as the day she had buried her mother and opened her eyes. Harriet needed her now. Meghan straightened her shoulders and placed her hand on Harriet's shoulder. No one should go through this alone.

~

The first thing Darcy saw when the curtain was drawn open, was Lachie laying on the bed, hooked up to machines. The nurse had said he was fighting, but he hadn't believed her. He tried to swallow down the emotion as he looked around the room. His mother sat in a traumatized heap on a shabby-looking chair. Meghan stood behind her, a reassuring hand on his mother's shoulder. He was surprised to see her, but grateful she was there and his mother had not been alone.

"He's not dead?" Darcy's voice was surprisingly calm even to him.

The women looked up at his arrival. Harriet clutched his hand and held onto him for dear life. "He's in a coma. We won't know the extent of his injuries until results come back and he wakes up."

"But he'll wake up?" Darcy looked at his mother, then at Meghan. Neither of them could answer the question. He looked down at his brother surrounded by machines and tubes.

Meghan touched his shoulder. "They're hopeful."

The compassion and love in her eyes was almost his undoing. He wanted to pull her into an embrace and accept the comfort she offered. But, he couldn't crumble right now. He had to remain strong for his Mum. With everything they'd been through—his father's death, Noah moving away, the drought—he didn't think she could take the death of a child.

"I need to walk." He glanced at his mother before slipping around the curtain. He needed to move, to scream, to stop thinking. There was nothing left but to pace the hospital's hallway while they waited for the news that might shatter their world.

Meghan followed him out.

"I was so scared we would lose him. The whole flight here I was preparing myself to plan a funeral." He looked blankly ahead, still in a state of shock.

"I'm sure he will be fine." She squeezed his hand. He hadn't even realised she had been holding it. He stopped suddenly and looked at her properly. "I'm glad you're here. Did Mum call you?"

She nodded. "I was waiting for your call and got hers instead. I was so frightened." She glanced around the corridor. "This place reminds me of when Mum died."

He pulled her into his arms and they clung together, her head cradled against his chest. "I'm sorry. This is all my fault. I should've told him sooner."

"This was about us?"

Darcy pulled back and looked into her face. "He got my phone. He saw the messages and our photos. He got angry and we had an argument."

"It's okay. It'll work out. Somehow." She clung to him.

"I should have known this would happen." He stiffened as he realised he couldn't have it all; he had to choose between his family and Meghan. Everything had been leading to this one decision. Guilt sliced through him like a dirty axe. He never should have gone to Meghan. He never should have betrayed his brother. This was his punishment. To be loved for a wonderful but brief time and then have to give it up.

"This is my fault. He might die and it will be because of me. Because I wanted you." His voice came out louder than he expected and she flinched. She wasn't expecting this. He was going to hurt her and it was the last thing he wanted to do.

Damn it. Did he have to hurt everyone he loved? First Lachie, now Meghan.

Emotion ached in his throat. "We can't be together anymore. I have to focus on Lachie now."

She stood still and stared at him for a long moment, her bottom lip trembling. His fingers ached to touch her. But he knew if he did, he would never be able to let her go.

Covering her face with her hands, she sobbed. She was falling apart in front of him. He had promised to protect her. But it turned out he was the one she needed to be protected from.

Her sobbing slowed and she finally looked up at him. Her eyes puffy and red. "No one can break my heart like you can."

"I'm sorry," he whispered.

Her shoulders slumped and her jaw clenched. She opened her mouth to say something but, nothing came out. Instead she turned and fled.

His chest ached and his vision blurred. Meghan was gone. Feeling as though his last breath had been pulled from his lungs, he finally lost control of his emotions and dropped to his knees as soul-deep sobs escaped him. He let the feelings swirl and envelop him for a few minutes. He deserved to feel the full extent of his suffering.

～

The house was suffocating hot when Meghan pushed

open the door. Her cheeks were still damp and her nose still running. Her lungs throbbed from all the sobbing.

She walked directly to her room and threw herself on the bed.

The bed she had shared with Darcy.

Sensing her need for comfort, Banjo jumped up on the bed next to her and she curled around him, clinging to him fiercely.

This was all her fault. The McGuire family must be cursing the day she entered their lives. Lachie was on death's door and Darcy couldn't even look at her.

The familiar stirrings of despair rose up from the dark recesses of her mind. No one loved her. No one wanted her. No one cared for her. She could have had a family, a home. But she had thrown it away. Now she would be alone forever.

She clutched the pillow against her face and sobbed for hours. She mourned the loss of the love she had with Darcy. For the relationship she had enjoyed with Harriet. She cried for Lachie, who lay helpless in that cold hospital. She cried for her parents who were the only people who had ever truly loved her, and finally, Meghan cried for herself.

CHAPTER 19

*I*t was an anxious wait for Harriet and Darcy, but finally, two days later, Lachlan McGuire woke up from his coma. The relief Darcy felt at his brother's recovery was dampened only by the ache he still felt for Meghan.

Although dreadfully tired and sore, Lachie's test results were positive and there would be no long-term damage to his brain or spine. In time and with substantial rehabilitation he would be able to resume his normal active life.

"He's okay. He's really okay." Harriet exclaimed to Darcy in the cafeteria over lunch.

"He'll think he's invincible now. Like Superman or something." Darcy let out a shaky laugh. His hands trembled slightly. The knowledge was still sinking in. He had almost given up hope after the first day, but his brother had surprised everyone and made it through.

"You should call Meghan. She'll want to know."

He squirmed uncomfortably in his seat. Could he rub his hands over his face, shielding out the pain of her? Then the following sentence supports his actions.

"Darcy. What have you done?" She placed her hand on her son's and waited for him to look at her.

"Meghan and I..." He bit his lips, struggling to find the right words. He wondered if she had suspected their affair. She had never asked, even when he had come back alone, swollen-eyed after speaking to Meghan that day in the hospital.

"Did you break up with her?" Harriet's question was slow and careful.

Darcy's cheeks burned. His mother tilted her head slightly and gave him a small smile which said of-course-I-knew.

"I've betrayed him. And you." Darcy rubbed his head which had started throbbing. "I had to end it."

She rubbed his back. "You certainly didn't meet under the best circumstances. But even I could see that you had a connection far stronger than she had with Lachie. I was proud of her when she left him. That took strength."

Darcy frowned at his mother. "She hurt him. I hurt him."

"Lachie usually gets what he wants. He hasn't had to struggle like you and Noah, especially where your father was concerned. He's spoilt. I take the blame for it. But he also needs to grow up and learn how to forgive."

"He won't forgive me. He told me to leave the station."

"That was before the accident. He almost died. He might think differently now," Harriet said.

"Will you talk to him? He listens to you."

Harriet nodded in reply. "Give it some time. Time always helps."

"Thanks, Mum." He smiled back at her, admiration and respect filling his heart for the woman he proudly called his mother. She didn't hate him. She believed Lachie would forgive him. Perhaps there was hope that they could all go back to Brigadier Station and life could resume the way it had before Meghan had ever set foot on their dusty patch of earth. They could be a family again. He could have his brother back. That would be enough.

Darcy thought about Meghan and his heart ached. He could never have her again. That was asking for too much. He would be happy to go back to his quiet life as long as he had his family.

Darcy needed to get back to the station. Work needed to be done there and he was of little use at the hospital. But first he needed to see his brother alone.

Lachie was laying on his back, his bed propped up slightly. A bright white bandage wrapped firmly around his chest, another on his arm. His face was black and blue with bruises and cuts. The sheet covered his legs but Darcy imagined they were just as bruised.

Lachie looked over warily as he approached.

"Hi. How are you?" Darcy stood at the foot of the bed taking in the sight of this battered man.

"Nine lives you know. Like a cat." Lachie laughed but winced in pain. Darcy sat next to him in a tattered chair and studied the machines monitoring him. Lachie had always seemed invincible, full of life. It was a shock to see him in this state. But better like this than in a coffin.

"I'm so sorry. I never meant to hurt you. This is all my fault." He blurted the words out, needing to get the apology off his chest whether it was accepted or not.

"This is my fault." Lachie waved at himself. "I can be stupid when I drink and this is where it got me." He took a breath. "I shouldn't have driven the quad. I'm damn lucky it didn't kill me."

"You are lucky. But I betrayed you. You're my brother. I never set out to love her, though. I tried not to." His voice hitched as he spoke.

"Being in here really makes you think about things. I thought a lot about Meghan." Lachie's mouth was tense. "I was so angry when she left. I never dreamed she would leave me."

"She didn't want to hurt you. She just couldn't do it." It was hard speaking about her. Thinking about her.

"We weren't suited; I can see that now." Lachie caught his brother's eye. "You and her make more sense in a way I'll never understand."

Flickers of hope started in Darcy's chest, but he didn't dare say a word.

Lachie turned his face away. "I still have to get used

to the idea. But I don't want to be the reason you aren't together."

Darcy let out a breath he hadn't realised he was holding. "Thanks, that means a lot. But I broke up with Meghan and I really don't think she would ever take me back."

Lachie shrugged. "I'm not going to give you advice on women. Obviously, I don't know enough about them."

Darcy patted his brother's arm gently. "Thanks Lachie. You're a good guy."

Lachie squirmed. "Be a bit weird if she becomes my sister-in-law."

His eyes wide, his mind buzzing with possibilities, Darcy turned to gaze out the window. The sun was shining, the day was suddenly filled with possibility. Maybe it wasn't too late to win Meghan back. If Lachie could forgive him for this huge betrayal, maybe Meghan could forgive him for breaking her heart. It was worth a try. He loved her more than anything else. His heart ached for her. Maybe she would turn him down but he had to try. He had never had anything worth fighting for before. But their love was worth fighting for now.

CHAPTER 20

J'll meet you at the airport at seven then?" Meghan asked into her mobile as she threw clothes haphazardly into a cardboard packing box.

She was surrounded by packing boxes and bubble wrap. The removalists were busy loading her furniture into the truck.

In the early hours of that horrible night, she had decided it was time to take charge of her life. She had let others dictate where she lived and what she did for too long. She had to take charge of her own life. While her mother had been alive she had stayed close, but there was nothing holding her to Townsville anymore. A simple online check had shown a need for vet nurses in Rockhampton working at a large animal clinic. Perfect. She had been offered the job after a ten-minute phone conversation. Within the week her life had changed. The truck would leave her house by 6 p.m. and she was due on a flight at 7.30 p.m.

"Are you really sure about this?" Jodie's voice came from the speaker on her phone. Her friend would drive her to the airport. They would say their goodbyes there.

"I need to make my own life." Meghan's voice was quietly confident. "The job sounds great. Lots of horse work."

"Okay." Jodie sighed. Meghan was not going to be talked out of it. Rockhampton wasn't that far. No farther than Julia Creek, only you went south down the coast instead of the outback road.

"I gotta go. These boxes aren't going to pack themselves. I'll see you tonight." She clicked off the call and reached for the tape. Every closed box was like another plank boarding up her past. This would be a fresh start. She would be more confident and outgoing. Make some new friends and see more of the country. Go see some more campdrafts.

She shook her head. Don't go there.

Meghan shunned thoughts of Darcy every time they threatened to surface. He was a part of her past now. He had made his choice and would not change his mind.

She wondered if Lachie had woken up yet. If he had died she expected it would have made the news. It wouldn't make any difference to her life though. That door was firmly closed now.

She gazed over at the bookcase. Only one framed photo was left. The cherished picture of she and her mother had been taken just weeks before the accident that had claimed her mother's life. She stared at her mother's happy smile and waited for the usual clenching feeling in her heart to come as it always did when thinking of her mother. But it didn't come.

She touched the picture. "I love you, Mum."

Her mother, so like her daughter in looks and personality, gazed back from the frame. "Was this what you wanted for me? To take charge of my life?"

As if in answer there was a knock on the door. Banjo looked up from his curled-up position on the cool tiled floor and gave an inquisitive bark.

Expecting it to be a removalist with a question about what was going she just sang out, "In here."

"Meghan." His voice rooted her to the spot.

When she finally spoke, her voice was as small and tight as though she had forgotten to keep breathing. "Darcy."

She turned her gaze to him and studied him as though he were a ghost who might suddenly disappear. He was wringing his hands together.

"What's with the truck?" His eyes never left her face.

"I'm moving." Long seconds passed as the tension between them grew. When he didn't answer she picked up a box and idly moved it to the table.

"Lachie woke up," He finally said. "He's going to be okay."

Her legs sagged as relief flooded through her. "Thank God."

Darcy took a step toward her but she threw up a hand stopping him. "You've told me now. You should go."

"That's not the reason I came. Not the only reason anyway." He ran a hand through his hair. "I love you, Meghan. I want you back."

"What!" She stuttered the words, sure she was imagining this.

"I'm sorry I hurt you. Lachie's alright with us being together. Or he said he will be. We can be together." The quiet pleading in his voice was her undoing.

She clutched at her throat.

Darcy stepped toward her and held out his hand.

She studied his calloused palm and her fingers itched to touch him. She gazed back at his face. His eyes pleaded with her.

Banjo brushed past her legs and plonked down on her feet. Meghan looked down at the dog who studied her for a moment before turning his head to Darcy.

"Come back with me." His voice was soft and mellow. "We belong together."

The truth of his words caressed her and all doubt disappeared from her thoughts. They belonged together. They were stronger together.

Banjo jumped aside as Meghan closed the distance between herself and Darcy. She placed her hand in his.

She caught a glimpse of his elated smile before his lips took hers. Hungry and all consuming. He used his mouth to tell her all she needed to know. He would love her forever. He would never hurt her again.

They could overcome anything. As long as they were together.

CHAPTER 21

Meghan scanned the landscape, finding little but dirt, bleached grass and stubborn trees. Although it was two hours since they had left Brigadier Station, the drought ravaged countryside still looked the same. This was the Australian outback she had fallen in love with. The smells, heat and colours were all things she knew she couldn't live without. City people didn't know what they were missing.

Darcy finally turned the ute off the sealed road and entered under a finely carved iron arch with the words "Arabella Plains" carved into it.

"What a pretty name." Meghan smiled, carefree and happy.

Now that their relationship was out in the open Meghan was looking forward to taking the next step with Darcy and putting the past behind them. His relationship with his brother was still strained so he kept his distance, staying in the ringers' quarters with

Meghan, while Lachie recuperated in the house under Harriet's watchful eye.

Meghan spent all of her time with Darcy, working the station. She was particularly excited about today's adventure which included looking at some horses for sale.

The ute clattered over a cattle grid towards a sprawling complex of buildings, ringed by a deep gully of thick eucalypt trees.

Pulling up in an empty shed, she climbed down from the ute and looked around. The afternoon sun was painting the rugged trees, blond grass and rusty dirt with colour. It was beautiful and so spacious it seemed to stretch to eternity.

"Are they expecting us? I can't see anyone." It was eerily quiet for a working station.

"They are expecting us but no one is meeting us here." He grinned mischievously and took her hand in his. They walked a short distance near the building and were greeted by the most magnificent tropical garden she had ever seen. Palm, cycads and colourful bougainvillea abounded in a chaotic sort of beauty. Instead of dry, dusty earth, lush green grass carpeted the garden.

Meghan bent and touched its softness.

"It's an oasis. Absolutely stunning." She gazed appreciatively taking it all in. The centrepiece were proud rosebushes standing tall and full. Their multitude of white, pink and red blossoms shinning in the sunlight.

As she approached their perfume assaulted her

senses. She stood still and closed her eyes, letting the aroma cleanse her soul.

Darcy's warm arms surrounded her and she leant into his solid embrace.

"The owners have already moved." He whispered, his tantalizing breath near her ear. "This station is for sale and it's within our budget."

"Seriously?" She turned in his arms and saw the hopeful look in his eyes.

"I thought it would make a good stud farm. We could run some cattle and sheep too, but we could focus on the horses."

She turned to the buildings which were all in need of a paint job and some minor repairs from what she could see. "Have you looked inside? Do you know how much work there is to do?" Although she already knew the answer. Darcy was nothing if not thorough.

He took her hands in his and kissed both palms. "The house needs a bit of renovation and a woman's touch. The main bedroom has an en-suite and there are three rooms for the kids."

"Kids?" She giggled.

"I'd like to have some kids running around." He smiled back.

She bit her lower lip. "Me too."

"There's also a room with a view to this garden. It would make a good art studio."

"Really?" Excitement thrummed through her at the thought of being able to paint with this garden as inspiration. "I love it and I love you."

"I love you, Meghan. I promise to protect you and give you the best life I possibly can." He kissed her gently before reaching into his back pocket. To her surprise and delight, he presented her a small fabric case.

She took a deep breath as he opened it to reveal a large, square, pink stone, set on a simple gold band. It sparkled in the sunlight.

"Marry me?"

"Yes! Nothing in the world would make me happier." She threw her arms around his neck and kissed him.

Finally releasing her, he placed the ring on her finger. It was a perfect fit. She studied its simple perfection.

"It's a pink sapphire. My great-grandfather found it fossicking in central Queensland. He had it made into this ring for his fiancé. It's been passed down ever since." Darcy explained.

"Was it Harriet's?"

He nodded. "I asked her why she didn't give it to Lachie to give to you. She never answered me at the time, but I think she always knew you were meant for me, not him."

She gazed into his sea blue eyes. "And you were meant for me."

"I love you, Meghan." He picked her up around the waist and spun her around. She squealed with delight, knowing that this time, she would marry the right man for the right reasons.

Thank you so much for reading The Brothers of Brigadier Station. I hope you enjoyed Darcy and Meghan's journey to love. For more information about me and my books, including the inspiration behind my stories, how I help other authors, and plenty of other fun stuff visit my website. If you'd like to know when my next release becomes available, plus gain access to exclusive content, news and giveaways, please sign up to my newsletter via my website and social media:

www.facebook.com/sarahwilliamswriter
www.twitter.com/SarahW_Writer
www.sarahwilliamsauthor.com

Help others find their next read by leaving a review of this novel on your favourite book website.

Keep an eye out for the rest of the Brigadier Station series. Lachie and Noah will be waiting…

ACKNOWLEDGMENTS

To Kelly, Claire, Helen and Annie, thank you for believing in me and this story.

Thank you to everyone at the Romance Writers of Australia for your support and resources.

A big thank you and much love to my family for all their support and for putting up with me while I write. I love you all.

A special thank you to Rachael and Anthony for all the time and effort you put in helping me research and plan this series. Without you this book wouldn't have its authenticity.

And to you, dear reader. Thank you for choosing this book to read. I know there are many other distractions and entertainment options available these days, so thank you for joining Meghan, Darcy and me on this journey.

ABOUT THE AUTHOR

Sarah Williams spent her childhood chasing sheep, riding horses and picking Kiwi fruit on the family orchard in rural New Zealand. After a decade travelling, Sarah moved to tropical North Queensland to enjoy the heat and humidity and to work with Crocodiles.

When she's not absorbed in her fictional writing world, Sarah is running after her family of four kids, one husband, two dogs and a cat. She also runs her own small press publishing house and supports her peers to achieve their publishing dreams.

Sarah is regularly checking social media when she really should be cleaning.

To receive updates and free books, sign up for her mailing list

You can find her online at:
www.sarahwilliamsauthor.com

Made in the USA
Monee, IL
16 June 2022